Tales From The Tower
Inklings Year One

Copyright © 2017 by Inklings Press
All rights reserved. This book or any portion thereof
may not be reproduced or used in any manner whatsoever
without the express written permission of the publisher
except for the use of brief quotations in a book review.
Follow Inklings Press on Twitter @InklingsPress

*Dedicated to all those who supported Inklings Press in our first year
– our friends, family, reviewers and especially our readers.*

Here's to many more years!

Table of Contents

Foreword: The first Inklings..................6

Tales From The Tavern Foreword..................10

The Bear-Trap Grave..................14

True Story..................40

Battle at Veldhaven..................68

Silver Horn..................96

A Taste For Battle..................114

Tales From The Mists Foreword..................130

The Chickcharney..................134

Bone Peyote..................154

The Pillar of Hendarac..................182

Beast..................202

The Server of Souls..................220

Afterword..................236

4

Foreword: The first Inklings
By Leo McBride

You hold in your hand something we never thought would come to be.

Let's talk a little history. In the summer of 2015, a bunch of writers were kicking around ideas. Heck, let's call them – us – what we were. Hopeful writers. We were plugging away on our writing, some on novels, some on short stories. We were a ball of energy, like one of those fireworks ready to go off sending sparks whizzing off in a bunch of different directions.

Then a simple question – no, a challenge – came to be put forward. Why don't we publish it ourselves? Suddenly, there was one direction everyone was pulling in.

The first book published was Tales From The Tavern. It came under the imprint of Inklings Press, a name pulled from the Inklings group that we called our little writing collective in tribute to a much more famous gang of authors. You may have heard of them.

Our line-up boasted Brent A. Harris, Ricardo Victoria, Alei Kotdaishura and Matthew Harvey. Oh, and me, bringing up the rear.

We told tales of fantasy, we told tales of magic, we told tales in which the most daring thing might just have been showing our work to the world for the first time. Like the wizards and warriors in our stories, we dared.

In time for Halloween that year, we produced a horror-themed second volume, Tales From The Mists. Morgan Porter joined the roster for that collection.

To our delight, people read the books. To our astonishment, they liked them. To our wonder, they kicked off a series of books that now includes authors from far beyond the group that started it all, scattered around the world. We have visited the farthest edges of the galaxy in the sci-fi collection Tales From The Universe, we have watched our world take very different paths in the alternative history anthology Tales From Alternate Earths, and most recently we have soared into the world of science fantasy in Tales of Wonder.

Each of those books has appeared in electronic form, e-books, filling up Kindles and Kobos, iPads and I don't know what else around the world. But we wanted to go a step beyond that. We wanted to put our words in print, in physical form, and to start that off, we wanted to return to the beginning. To here. To the pages you hold in your hand.

We include the original forewords to each of the collections, both Tales From The Tavern and Tales From The Mists, and at the back of the book, you'll find more information about each of the writers – where to find them on social media, where to learn more about their other work.

It took a great deal of daring on the part of the authors featured here to take this leap, to take this step into the world of writing. Each is stronger and bolder because of it, and I urge you if you enjoy their work here, well... you've got something special awaiting in future collections.

Enjoy. And, if I might offer one piece of advice? Always be bold enough to make that leap.

Tales From The Tavern Foreword By Ricardo Victoria

As with most stories, our tale starts with rejection. It's truly the most clichéd event in a writer's life. But it's also the most common spur to make you work harder.

Little did Stephen, Brent and I imagine how this anthology, the first of many, would be created out of our conversation about success in the modern publishing world. Thinking back on it, none of us could have thought how this would be possible nine years ago when we met at a wargaming club at Loughborough University, while playing at a Heroclix tournament (by the way, Brent & Stephen, I still want that rematch). And here we are, with our nascent project that evolved from a self-published short story anthology to the seeds of our own editorial label.

Mind you, this is not a vanity project born of rejection, but instead a project born out of love and respect to the written word, facilitated by the modern possibilities of e-publishing.

It is a pooling together of our resources, as writers, editors, designers, and readers with a critical eye towards improving each other's works.

In that regard, we are aiming to follow the spirit of the group of writers and professors that give name to our group: The Inklings, a club of writers based at Oxford University featuring the likes of J.R.R. Tolkien and C.S. Lewis.

We work to help each other improve our craft, to create interesting stories, and to not only grow as writers ourselves, but to develop and nurture future writers.

And that's why we are here, putting together this anthology, with the help of friends, the support of our wives, fiancées and significant others who patiently endure our rants about the frustrating but rewarding nature of writing. These five stories are the result of an open call to friends who want to write and help them to get a foot in the door of the profession as well as push us out of our comfort zones – especially for two of us writing in our second language.

Now, why did we choose Tales from the Tavern as the title of the anthology? Simple, most of us met in the UK and there is nothing more quintessentially British than sharing our daily shenanigans over a pint of beer at the local pub, not unlike many fantasy characters do in books and roleplaying campaigns. And while we are now based in four different countries, we keep doing the same thanks to the possibilities of the social networks. Of course, some of us changed the beer for rum, but that's another story. We shared these tales among us and now, with you, our readers.

In our opening story, The Bear-Trap Grave, Brent A. Harris, fan of alternative history - and who is approaching publication of his American history novel - examines the meaning of friendship for people isolated from civilization in a maudlin story from the edges of a fantasy realm.

True Story, by Alei Kotdaishura, portrays how often the official version of an epic event rarely has any similarity with what actually happened, which makes us realize that people, especially in fantasy realms, tend to embellish the truth a little over their feats.

Matthew Harvey, who is an RPG aficionado with the ability to tinker with any system to the point of actually breaking it, brings us a more traditional fantasy story in the form of Battle at Veldhaven, a real treat of the genre.

Silver Horn by Ricardo Victoria - yes, that's my last name, not my middle name, thank you for asking - is a more comedic take of the traditional heroic quest is presented, with the aim of bringing a smile to the reader.

Finally, A Taste for Battle, by Leo McBride, uncovers the aftermath of a drunken rant by a charming rogue that ends with him and his friend in a rough spot against an invading army.

In closing, thank you for choosing to buy this book. We hope you enjoy the stories contained here as much as we enjoyed writing and critiquing them. And if you really liked them, please pass your praise along to your friends and family and leave a positive comment in the reviews. If everything goes according to our evil plans of world domination, this will be but the first of many other anthologies and novels that we hope to bring to you, but it is not possible without your support. Thank you.

The Bear-Trap Grave
By Brent A. Harris

I preferred to be alone. Solitary. Me against the wild. Other people bothered me. When I would go into villages, on necessary business, I was sometimes asked why I didn't at least have a dog to keep me company. After all, dogs make great companions for skinners like me. I just ignored them.

I ignored everyone, except for Bunny Logan. Occasionally, we would team-up on a hunt, to increase our profits. On one such occasion, I heard him hollerin' for help. He never hollered for help. It was what I liked about him. He was quiet and kept his distance.

His dog and I even got along. He was perhaps the closest thing I'd call to having a friend, though I would never tell him that.

His call for help startled me. I ran deeper into the greenwood—trees whose sharp, thin needles remained green even through the harshest of snows—toward the sound of his pleas. I struggled hard, heart pumping, my canteen of silvershine slapping my ass despite my coverings of thick brown furs as I trudged through the snow.

I spied him hunched over, his back to me, furiously digging through the snow, and then pulling at something as hard as he could.

He stopped for a moment, as if trying to regain his strength and he yelled for me, "Fowler…we need you!"

I sludged through some more thick snow, snaking through a thin path between wide trunks to avoid the stabbing-green needles, till I saw what he was doing down there like that. When I saw his face, it was in tears and he was straining with all his might.

Why didn't I have a dog? Dogs die. I couldn't handle the loss. I wouldn't handle seeing my companion down there in the snow like that, muzzle in a rusted trap, suffocating, frantically dying…well, that there might well set me off… again. And I don't need that. Better to stay detached. People are pretty horrible.

"Stop," I yelled at him. He'd never free York from the trap by trying to pull it apart. But, it didn't make sense for him to stop. After all, he was trying to free his companion. The mouth-trap kept York's muzzle closed tight. It was wickedly clever in its design. There's food down in it and when an animal grabs it up, the trap shuts around its jaws. York was whimpering. His jaw looked broken.

York's natural tan and black fur coat remained deathly still around his chest—she couldn't breathe right. York looked on the verge of defeat. And so did Bunny.

"Stop," I yelled at him again. I shoved him to the side, so he'd get the point. "Those springs are too heavy, there's no way in Dystanpia you'd tear that open." He didn't hear me. Or, rather, ignored me, I thought. In either case, York was dying. Time was precious. I took Bunny's place in front of the rusted contraption. Bunny looked at York through tear-welled black eyes.

My actions probably infuriated Bunny—seeing his dog like that and then seeing my almost casual response to it. After I shoved him over, I just plopped down on the snow and started taking my tan, leather boots off. While York whimpered, I unlaced the leather strap on one boot as I desperately recalled how this particular trap worked.

Skinners are hunters—not trappers. There are no traps allowed in all the Lost Kingdoms. Skinners stalk live prey, take them down, then skin 'em and sell the furs, meats, and bones to traders in the villages. If we didn't do that, people would starve. Of course, there are a few ignorant people out there who still used traps to catch food, rather than relying on us. They've caused more than their own share of problems for everyone.

I took a deep breath and then took my leather strap and thumbed it through one end of the coiled spring on the trap. This was hard to do in the snow with numbed fingers and York's own raspy, rhythmic breathing reminding me of how much time was passing. I was getting flustered, I worried I might let Bunny's dog die. He'll be sad if that happens. But, I managed it after a few failed attempts. I'm good—on occasion.

Then, I threaded the same leather into the coil at the opposite end of the trap. I pulled both sides of the leather taught, the springs closed in and half of the trap suddenly loosened. Yay me. I've got two of the four coils pulled back. Now, to do the other side.

Only now, York was excited. The trap was loosened just enough to let blood flow back into his muzzle, bringing the big dog all sorts of pain. As he started thrashing about, he got too excited... and passed out from asphyxiation.

Bunny didn't seem to like that reaction.

"What did you just do?" It wasn't a question. It was an accusation.

People, I swear—not very trusting. I didn't even bother to calm Bunny down. He could flail around if he wanted too. If I didn't get my other lace off and into the trap...York wouldn't be waking up.

Six years later

The sign on the tavern simply read, 'The Tavern'. But there was room on the sign for one more word. If you looked carefully, you could see where, 'Trapper's' used to be. I walked into the old Trapper's Tavern.

Springtime had left mud on my boots from the wet, winding mountain paths. I wiped the mud off onto the boot-bar as disdainfully as you would if you had stepped in dog droppings. I hated the spring. I'm down to only the lightest of furs. My greying, dusky hair was shorter too. I even had to trim off my beard. Now it was just stubble.

As a skinner, the springtime made it hard to sell my wares. Furs didn't sell when you didn't need 'em. As for meats— well, the forests were so plentiful with squirrels that they'd jump out of trees and run into your boiling pots if you'd left your doors open. Wasn't much call for work.

The tavern was less than crowded. I wasn't the only skinner who didn't like spring. The lack of skinnin' meant lack of coin, which one needed to trade for drink and the finer bits of life. The fireplace went unused. The beds upstairs were probably empty. Which meant the pretty tavern wenches were all in the village, wasting away, caring for their children or some other such nonsense.

This all meant that it didn't take long to spot the reason for my being here: Bunny sat at a bench behind a neglected table. On it, an empty glass of silver-shine sat in solitude. York, gray as all get-out, with her crooked muzzle, panted by her master. She's a good dog.

Bunny's gonna be sad when she departs. It wouldn't be long now. Bunny lifted his empty glass when he saw me. In a gruff voice, riddled with age, he said, "I was wondering if you were going to come, Fowler." In the past, he'd rise when I came in. But that was six years ago. Ever since he lost his lower left leg in the Second Elf War, he'd been a bit slower. The leg was wooden now, but he was no less deadly—if you waited for him to hobble over to you. "Now that you're here, you can top me off again, unless your coin is running lower than mine."

I placed two pieces on the table—a drink for both of us. He didn't know that was the last of it. I might have been a better skinner than Bunny, but only because I still had both my legs.

Besides, it's my fault he was down an appendage. He didn't know that either.

A while later, a stringy boy came by to take my coin. That was all that was left in the villages. Young boys and their mothers. Ain't never heard anyone says they like war, yet there's always one to be had. Didn't make sense. But, at least it had kept me in business.

Without skinners, women and boys in the villages starved. Sure, there was a few lady-skinners, but we seldom came across them. More common were young boys, who had been too young to die in the last war. "Don't worry," I always told 'em, "you'll get your chance to die in the next war soon enough."

The boy returned with two tins in hand. He plopped 'em on the table with a clang. Sticky liquid poured out. I frowned, wanting to tell the boy that I'd just paid for what he spilt, but I let the moment pass. Chances were, I'd cause more trouble than it was worth. Bunny and I shared a simultaneous swig of weak 'shine. Still, my stomach was empty, so even the watered down liquid felt good.

My stomach didn't have to be empty. I was a skinner, after all. But, if I was to tell you the truth, unless I was ingesting chewy squirrel meat, it was too much of a bother. I could track an elk, or a pheasant, or whatever, and do my thing. But, afterwards, what would I do with the left-over meat? I'm just one person.

Bunny and I examined each other in misanthropic silence. We were both awkward at this. Still, he had set this meeting up for some reason. I waited for him to speak. Finally, after another, long, hard swallow, he drained his tin of 'shine, slammed it down, and let out a belch. That was his signal that we were ready to get to business.

Bunny said, "I got an opportunity for you, a chance to make some coin for the lean spring ahead."

"Go on," I eagerly listened.

"There's a rogue bear out roaming the mountains of a tiny village not too far from here."

Already, I was bored. Bears get a bad reputation. Their stories were always overblown. People live in fear of them, when really, people are just being ignorant. "Bears roam. They hunt, and eat dragonfish as they head upstream during spawning season. I once saw a clever bear wait on top of a two-foot waterfall, mouth open.

The dragonfish would fly out of the water, straight into its jaws." I shook my head and petted York. She licked my hand. "Bears are like us, they keep to themselves."

"Not this one," he said. "Not according to the whispers coming out of the Ghost Woods. This bear is angry. He's rampaging. He's killing. He's making it impossible for skinners to bring food to the village.

They are starving. It's your chance to profit."

"Once I kill myself a bear?."

"Uh-huh."

I got up to leave, the chair scraped against the warped(,) wooden floor. If there'd been any customers in the tavern, they would have stopped at the noise.

Bunny tried to keep me there, he said in a raised voice, "This bear's twelve-foot tall."

That was not the right thing to say to me. No bear was that big. I tell Bunny, "Those are just whispers."

I turned to leave.

He stomped his peg leg down hard on the floor. It thundered and echoed like the bellow of a dragon down a valley. York stood, ears up. "It's not my business to make such exaggerations. If I say there's a bear out there, I mean it. I stake my reputation on it, what it's worth." Bunny pointed to his wooden protrusion. "Besides, you owe me your ears. I gave you my leg."

My shoulders slumped. Apparently, he did know that it was my fault. But I shrugged it off and unleashed a comeback of my own,

"People make their own problems. You chose to come after me during the heaviest of the fighting, you are the one who lost your leg. You can blame the Elf that sliced it off, if you want. Not me." It wasn't my finest moment.

"Fine." He threw his hands up in the air. "I've always known you had a problem with being decent. But I thought that I was an exception. Don't know why." I stood there silently. He reached over and grabbed my drink. He drained the tin. I regretted my words now more than ever.

York sat as I returned to the table. Bunny continued, "Let me switch to a language we both understand. These starving villagers sit on a rock of aurium. Nice, shiny aurium. Coin has never been their problem. But this bear is. They are offering a bag full of the shiny stuff to get rid of the bear."

"How big a bag are we talking?" I asked skeptically.

He whispered a number. My jaw dropped. Even in numerical form, I couldn't fathom it. I said in shock,

"That's a real big bag." That was the problem with us skinner types. We could be bought. But, I suppose in a way, everyone could.

Some are just more translucent about it than others. Perhaps those are the honest ones.

I sat silently for a bit, wishing Bunny hadn't drained my glass, wishing I had enough coin to buy another. I already knew I was going to go. It was worth at least checking out.

"Kill an elk, you're fed for a week," Bunny started off with the old adage again before changing it. "Kill a rampaging bear, fill your stomach with free drinks for as long as people tell the story."

I grunted in agreement. We're fine folk, Bunny and I.

"I'm sorry about your…" I stumbled. I pointed to his stump. I don't know how to apologize.

"I went out after you, 'cause you saved my dog. I lost my leg on account of it. But, I still got York here…" He petted the dog. York seemed happy, "…and you're still around. I guess I'd say my leg for my dog and a friend is a fair trade."

I grumbled silently under my breath. Bunny was not my friend—I suppose. But, if the bear really was the problem he said it was, then it'd be convenient to have a spare…hand. I chuckled at my own morbid humor, though it certainly wasn't funny. The guy had already lost a leg.

"Of course, I'm gonna expect a free drink tossed my way every now and then, on account of me passing along this information."

"You're gonna get more than that, friend," I said.

He cocked his head sideways in confusion as he circled his craggy finger around the rim of his empty tin, "How so?"

"You're coming with me." Honestly, Bunny would only slow me down. But I was in no hurry anyway. I had a hard time believing his story. I just wanted him there so I could tell him, "I told you so."

He ignored his bow and arrows as he said, "If you hadn't noticed, I'm short a leg. Won't be able to keep up. Won't be able to help you none."

"Good," I said, smiling. "We're more likely to get attacked by a mountain cat than a bear. When that happens, I'll offer your leg up as a scratching post."

When I said people created their own problems, I didn't realize it applied to me. But, after seeing how there was a twelve-foot brown bear breathing in my face, I understood my hypocrisy. I could've just said no. Problem solved. But here it was, and I was facing it alone. Bunny and York were nowhere to be found. Perhaps solitude was not the answer. I swallowed hard.

The journey didn't start off too bad. Like Bunny said, we weren't too far away. The biggest problem had been getting to the Ghost Wood. Every year, the leaves on the trees fell off. Every year, they returned. People said it was the magic of the Elves. I think, people are just fearful. Only magic I have ever seen an elf perform during two wars, was to slice through the men of our ranks. They did that well enough — which explained why we lost both times. I'm sure once we have grown more boys to men, there'll be a third war we can lose. The shortage of men was the only thing that kept the peace — and money in my pocket.

In any case, there were no paths into the Ghost Woods or paths in the forest that we saw. The ground was muddy with spring and the tree-branches bulbed and sprouted as new leaves returned to reclaim the dead. I could feel the air thinning as we trailed up the mountain past wisps of low-laying fog.

It was slow going, of course. York was old. Bunny was lame. I was in no rush. We'd been in the vicinity of the 'supposed' bear for three days now. It wasn't around. It didn't matter, there was ample food to hunt and enough of us to make a kill worthwhile. And maybe there'd be work in the village at the aurium deposits along the slow rivers.

I could learn to like it here. The air was cooler, I got to wear my coon-skin cap. There did seem something 'magical' to the place.

But, it was an enchantment, not a curse. The Ghost Woods were terribly named. There was no twelve-foot bear.

And that's when I slipped.

I'm sticking to the story that it was muddy. People slip in the mud.

It could happen to anyone. Unfortunately it happened to me, just as I crested a hill…and I slipped down the other side. York got young again and raced to the top, barking for me. I heard and witnessed part of it as I fell. I also heard Bunny calling me an old fool.

Harrumph. I'm grizzled, not old.

I tumbled down the damned hill, avoiding trees where I could, then splashed into the edge of a lake. I spied him…or her, before the bear spied me. I didn't know if this was our bear or not; it was in the water, nearly submerged. As soon as I splashed in, it snapped its neck around and saw me. A blood-rage shot out its eyes at me. It stood. Then it stood some more. Yup. It was indeed twelve-feet tall.

I wanted to yell, "I found it!" but my breath escaped me. I could smell hers. As I recoiled at her stink, I thought to myself that I'd never eat dragonfish again. She roared. With one swipe of her paw, she could have ended me, right there. Her claws were each as long as my hand, as sharp as my one hunting knife—she had twenty of them.

She swiped at me. It was a powerful blow, but it was wide. It was almost as if she were unfocused—swinging with anger alone. I didn't mind. I was still alive. But it also meant that the bear was unpredictable. I'd been skinnin' for a while now, I've hunted almost everything. And I've survived two wars. Retreat was the best option.

I pissed myself. Thankfully, I was already wet in the lake.

I scampered up the shore, like a crazed crab, trying to put some distance between me and Mrs Grumpy Grizzly. As I splashed about, I tried to assess my options: I had my hunting knife, which seemed pretty paltry, I had a tree-blade for firewood and I had my… I looked at the remains of my bow and I saw a couple of arrows floating by in the water. It didn't survive my tumble.

The bear took another swipe at me, growling as she swung her claws. I dodged that one. I dodged the next one, too. I wouldn't have survived all this time if I wasn't somewhat nimble or boasted some talent at this. Still, I know skill could smack against bad luck at any moment. It could be now. The bear reared up as if to charge me.

I stood on dry land. And I knew better than to climb a tree. Once, I climbed a rock outcropping to escape an enraged mother black-bear when her cubs thought I was a friendly playmate. The black-bear couldn't dig her claws into the flat stone. She'd eventually escorted her children away and left me there. This bear wasn't protecting any cubs. In truth, I didn't know what her problem was.

My only choice was to run up the hill I just tumbled down. I did so, but in a zig-zag pattern. It was a big bear, but she couldn't turn as swiftly as I could. As I raced away, I heard the metallic clanging of something dragging behind her, hitting each rock and branch. I couldn't tell what it was. Besides, I was kinda busy at that moment.

As I ran, I unhooked my knife. It felt so small in my hand. But, it was all I had. I also had no choice but to twist myself and throw the knife into the beast. It was not made for throwing, but I had to slow her down, otherwise, I would be food. And I was not made for eating. The pointy edge of the blade sailed toward the bear's eye.

But she turned and raised herself. It stabbed harmlessly into her shoulder. Still, it had to hurt, and she stopped for a moment, howling in agony. That was my cue to run faster, this time, straight up the hillside. Then, I reached for my tree-blade.

But, it seemed it didn't take much for her to catch up. With a burst of power, she was already over me.

York, bless that dog, jumped on her, and tore out a piece of her skin—a clump of brown fur hung bloody in her jaw. As the bear reared up, I took my tree-blade and buried it into her chest. Even though it lodged into her, it didn't seem to make it past her ribs.

Even so, she howled again, this time, jerking York off and hurtling her at a tree. I heard bones crunch as York smacked into it. York laid there, still. I hoped the poor dog wasn't dead. I would be sad.

The bear turned its attention directly toward me. I'd lost my last weapon, and the bear was still on top of me. I was as good as dead.

She raised her claws into the air, I turned, side facing the bear—I bunched up my fur-lined leather coat around my arm for what little protection it afforded me and waited for the inevitable.

The pain was excruciating. I'd been cut before. But this was five times worse. My skin was shredded, blood poured out. Every hair on my bare arm felt like it was on fire. I was in no shape to defend myself for its next attack. The beast raised its paw again.

I heard a thwip of an arrow to my right. It flew into the bear's neck. It stopped her. I looked over to see Bunny, but he was too far away to make out. Still, I called out to him, "Hey, couldn't you have maybe hobbled down a little faster?" It was nice to have a friend.

He answered with another arrow—it whipped by, striking the great bear in the chest. It would have been a kill-shot for any other beast. On her, it barely penetrated her thick fur. Even so, thick, black blood oozed from the wound. The bear let out a deafening growl. If I hadn't pissed myself in the lake, my fur would be more than just wet right then.

The bear decided to ignore me and charged in the direction of the new threat. There was no time to check my wound—with a painful grunt, I rose. My shoulder was shot. But at least I was in better shape than Bunny was about to be. I raced toward him.

As a skinner, I would have approached the bear just as Bunny had —I would have kept the Dystanpia away. Arrows were the preferred method to dispatch a creature, but they would have done me no good. We had one old, hurt dog, a guy with one leg, and me with my shredded shoulder, against this behemoth of a bear. Odds didn't look great. I saw it dragging something behind him as it ran Bunny down.

Luckily, Bunny was ready for her. He hailed from the south, where forests turn into jungles. His vine-cutter was out, the long blade angled up. It was dulled from use, but the bear provided plenty of momentum to overcome its lack of an edge. I heard the sick sound of skin slicing as Bunny met the bear.

I arrived just in time to see the bear topple over—right on top of Bunny. With what little might I had left, I broke into a sprint and barreled into the side of the bear with my good shoulder. The blow barely moved the beast, but it was enough to knock him off Bunny. I saw him on the ground, gasping for breath. But he looked otherwise unharmed.

The bear looked lifeless, but only for a moment. She was rising, before we had a chance to recoup. If the bear recovered before us, Bunny would be dead. I'm stupid, and I jumped on the damn bear to keep that from happening. Her fur was matted and smelt about as bad as a wet dog. As she lifted herself up over Bunny, I found the wound York left earlier and jabbed my fingers into the holes. The bear was mad, but she was mad before.

I told Bunny to clear out, but even before I got the words out, I could tell something was wrong, "Get up you old fool! Get up!"

He struggled and strained, for some reason he couldn't move. I didn't know why. I was still on top of the bear, being me. I was unable to get down to help. Bunny called out, in his same gruff voice, "He shattered the peg, it's stuck on something."

First off, the Bear is a 'she'. I already called it. Second, how'd Bunny get his leg caught? Th'at was not very helpful. "See the treecutter embedded into her chest?" I yelled from atop the bear in a croaked voice. "Grab it and cut yourself loose!"

The bear was trying to get me off of it. She was just about to succeed. Then, she let out a howl of fury. Bunny must have grabbed the blade. I saw him for a second, holding it in his hand, about to bring it down on his wooden leg.

Then the bear swiped down. I didn't see it coming, but the effect was brutal—Bunny's hand had all but disappeared. The tree-cutter flew away, off to Bunny's left—his fingers were still wrapped around it. My friend let out a chill cry—I somehow shared the pain.

My anger rose. I punched the bear in the wound and flew off her, heading toward the weapon. It was only a few paces away. I bent down and flicked his fingers off it and raced back toward the bear to end this. But, I wasn't fast enough. The bear brought her claws down on Bunny with a malicious, mauling, growl. I heard it. I even felt it. My insides wanted to come out. I knew Bunny was dead.

I don't even remember embedding my tree-cutter into the bear's skull. I don't know how I became slick with blood. Some of it was my own, from my shoulder. The rest of it must have come from the wounds of the great bear or when I held Bunny in my arms as I cried out.

York hobbled over, let out a mournful howl and licked his master's face.

I walked over to the lake and washed myself off. In my pack, I had honey and herbs and string to salve and sew my shoulder. I took a few moments for myself and then went back to Bunny and the bear. I didn't want to. But Bunny was my friend. I learned this too late and the realization makes me angry.

I started digging a hole by the lake. I didn't want any more animals getting a piece of him, and the ground was soft and muddy, easy for grave digging. I turned my focus to the bear. There was blood everywhere. We wounded her so much, but she still just kept at us. I wonder what would do that to a creature. After all, even beasts aren't born into violence. It's something learned from others.

After a moment of examination, I saw the answer—on the bear's left hind foot was a monstrous contraption of devious design. Its teeth were long and sharp, of cold iron, flaked with brown bits of rust. It rings around the bear's foot, each tooth produced its own swollen protrusion of cracked, dry blood and scabbed skin, rebroken with every morning dawn. That was the reason for the bear's rage. Bears eat dragonfish from the peaceful waters. Bears don't attack people of a quiet village—unless it was provoked.

I should have been furious. But for some reason, I was calm. I was still as the water on the lake. With practiced precision I skinned the bear, head to toe. Then, I dug another hole—a much larger hole.

With considerable effort, I heaved the beast down into its grave. I felt the earth shake as the bear hit the ground. I took the huge brown fur and wrapped Bunny in it. Despite York's protest, I lowered Bunny into the ground and covered him up. York laid forlornly on Bunny's grave.

It was nearly night by then. I laid against a tree next to York. She whimpered. Her cries sent me off to a deep sleep.

I awoke to find York licking me. It was the first time I had seen her off Bunny's grave. I rose and stretched. My shoulder was stiff and sore. I spied the outskirts of the village nestled into the rise of the mountain on the other side of the peaceful lake through thin fog.

There was rope in my pack. I took a sturdy branch and tied the rusted bear trap to it, then I jammed the marker into the soft earth. It was traps like these that started the first Elf War. It was this trap that killed my only friend.

I headed away from the village as quick as I could manage. I won't be going there. York walked with me, though I didn't know where I was headed. I ran my hand over her head as she licked my palm. She didn't have a whole lot of life left in her, but I'd be with her every step of the way.

True Story
By Alei Kotdaishura

It was a dark and stormy night, full of thunder and lightning which cast a luminescent glow–

"Please tell me you're not beginning your story like that," I groaned when Dad began. "It's so cliché!"

"Shush" he replied, "I know, but this is the way it happened."

While the wind howled in the trees and the icy rain fell mercilessly, every living being was hiding, waiting for the storm to break, hoping for it to pass without destroying their hiding places or their homes, leaving them drenched in the darkness.

Unfortunately, this was no common storm, for it had been conjured by a warlock so powerful and so terrible that people in the nearby towns only whispered about him and his evil deeds. Back then it was said that if you dared to call his name, he would turn up right beside you in an instant to kill you, thus referring to him as The Silver Warlock.

"Oh c'mon, Dad!" I said, with a hint of exasperation growing in my voice. "Of all the stories you want to tell you had to choose this one? Why do I even have to hear it again?"

"Well, you have heard the official version, son. Now you can hear the real one," replied Dad patiently. "But if you want, I can act it out to make it a bit more interesting for you."

"No, love," interrupted Mom abruptly through her usual smile. "No story-acting. Stick to the truth or I will keep interrupting you to correct the story. Hopefully our son will be patient with us."

It had been hard convincing my father to tell me the truth of one of his stories. I keep hearing the official version, but Mom and Dad usually whisper at home about not telling the whole story, so I finally gathered the courage to ask him and he agreed grudgingly.

"Alright, alright," Sighed Dad. "Since you insist, I will start again."

It was dark and stormy, but it wasn't night. It was midday but it didn't really matter, for you could have sworn it was midnight. The Silver Warlock did conjure the storm around the whole Silver Forest and the towns surrounding it. He did so in order to hide himself and make it difficult for anyone who tried to find him, as we found later.

We were young then, rather reckless and bursting with energy. I was twenty and your mother was eighteen. We kept challenging ourselves to beat impossible odds because we wanted to become heroes and have legendary stories, but so far all our deeds were a couple of pet rescues.

"Pet rescues?" I was astonished. Who could believe that heroes could begin by rescuing pets?

"Yeah," replied Dad. "Nothing worthy of a heroic title: some dragons hidden in caves that had to be returned and taken back to their owners, a poor manticore that was trapped in a swamp…"

"And the basilisk from that old witch, remember? I think that one was one of my favorites," added Mom with a reminiscing air. I had to manage not spitting my tea in shock, forcing myself to gulp it down. Who in their right minds would call those creatures 'pets'?

When we reached Silver Town, the townspeople were in turmoil. The storm had been raging for over a month and the people were hungry, angry and desperately wet. Everywhere in town there were pools of water as well as muddy and slippery streets. In some cases, roofs had even leaked so much that entire families had to move into other houses in order to keep themselves somewhat dry, leaving them with (not surprising at all) no mood for strangers.

We went into the inn and asked about a room. We were lucky, because after waiting in a queue behind a hydra charmer and a mage there was only one room left, big enough for the two of us and, even luckier, bug-free.

"Excuse me for interrupting" I had to say. "What is a hydra charmer?"

Mom rolled over her pretty golden eyes and answered, "It's like a snake charmer, with his flute and basket and so on," she explained, talking to me as if I was a simpleton, "but using baby hydras."

After we rested for a while, we went down to have what would be dinner if there were any daylight outside and ended up sharing our table with the mage. He was clean shaved and dressed in clean grayish clothes, almost white. He also seemed mature, but not very old.

"What weird weather, right?" I asked the mage as a manner of greeting.

He looked at us while he drank from his beer tankard, but didn't answer.

"I heard that the rain is caused by some magic spell and that it's been going on for a while. What do you think?" asked your mom. "I hope it isn't true. I couldn't stand being in this weather that long. Imagine how my gorgeous hair would look in the rain!"

The mage stared at her but still said nothing. Since he remained silent, we enjoyed our food and drink.

After we finished, the mage sighed contentedly and sat straight.

"Ap-parently yo-u guys kno-w no-thing." He confided to us.

We sat closer to him and paid attention to his words. His manner of speech beat down my eardrums, for he seemed to be cutting the words every two syllables and then made some guttural noises whenever he pronounced more than that. His accent was heavy and strange, making it difficult to understand him, making us grimace every time the mage spoke.

"All of this is the work of the Silver Warlock," he began. "He is hoping to stop his enemies from finding him before he finishes his newest weapon."

"What kind of weapon?" I asked intrigued. It sounded like an adventure.

"I don't know," he answered. "But whatever it is, it's worth drowning the whole county and the forest."

"Why are you telling us this?" I asked, suspicious of him but trying to contain my excitement.

"Because I think I know how to reach him, but I won't be able to do it by myself." He explained. "I'm a mage and I want to defeat him, but I will need protection during the trip to His lair. After all, I'm useless for physical tasks."

We looked at the mage and he was right, you know? He was scrawny and seemed like he wouldn't even be able to lift more than a couple of books, but his eyes seemed clever and I had a strange feeling.

My gut was winding, warning me. I was uneasy, but it could be because of the adventure awaiting us, or the thrill of rushing into the unknown.

"And the thought of this being a trap never crossed your mind?" I blurted, "You keep telling me to pay attention to any catches before accepting propositions from strangers."

Dad glared at me before answering.

"This is the reason why I warn you, kiddo." He replied before turning back to the story.

We stayed quiet, not knowing what to say. After a few minutes we looked at each other, reaching silent consensus and we turned to the mage.

"Alright," I told him. "We can be your companions, but we will want three quarters of the treasures."

The mage smiled and nodded.

"I leave in the morning; I want to finish this business quickly. Rest well." He said and left to his room.

Dad interrupted himself and gazed into the distance with a thoughtful expression on his face.

"He was mocking us when he accepted," he remarked suddenly.

"Yeah," Mom seemed somewhat disappointed. "We were a pair of fools."

"So there were no treasures" I stated, nodding. That I could understand.

"Nope, there were but…" started Mom and then changed her mind. "Ah, you'll see."

So we followed the mage's example and left to our room. We checked our traveling equipment (which wasn't much). I checked the weapons and verified they were sharp enough while your mom went to the innkeeper and asked him for food that could resist the heavy rain. We didn't know how many days it would take but it shouldn't be long. A festival was coming and we were already planning the celebration of our first heroic deed.

In what would be the morning hours, after we had rested and breakfasted, we met the mage at the inn entrance. He looked us over roughly and nodded with a gesture of passing approval and placed a magic enchantment on our lamps so they wouldn't extinguish, even in the wind and rain.

We left the inn and made our way out of town, which was full of muddy pools, so we kept slipping and sliding, taking us longer than we expected to reach the outskirts to the forest entrance, where the mage stopped under the town gate and waited for us to catch up. He seemed to know exactly where to step to avoid slipping and was faring better than us.

"Stop," I interrupted. "You're telling me that the older and scrawny-looking mage was actually more agile than two youngsters?"

"Yeah, that's correct." Dad nodded.

"Seeing it backwards, it's logical, you know?" interrupted Mom, "Although he did hurt our pride."

"Before we leave I was a bit rude yesterday," he said apologetically "and we haven't made our introductions yet. My name is Drack Eon."

We made our introductions and he nodded slightly and pointed to the forest while taking out and extending a folded piece of paper that didn't get wet, so we assumed it was magically protected.

"This is a map of the area," he explained. "I've been asking around in the towns and villages surrounding the forest and I've marked the most probable location of the Silver Warlock's lair. I used to live here years ago, so it shouldn't be that hard to find."

He checked his map and folded it back into his backpack.

"This way," he said and we followed him.

In the beginning, the road wasn't really that hard. I think the hardest part was, like getting out of town, evading the water pools that formed between the trees. That day was rather uneventful. Even the forest felt really peaceful, storm notwithstanding.

"But you found some angry animals on the way?" I interrupted, dismayed. It sounded like a rather boring story.

"Nope, all of them were hiding from the rain," replied Mom, matter-of-factly.

"No goblins, or trolls either?" I asked hopefully.

"Nope," replied Dad, bothered by the interruption. "It was a peaceful stroll in the forest... under the storm, of course."

The next day, Drack consulted his map again before we left. As we kept going deeper and deeper into the forest, the thunder and lightning made everything look even more eerie than it already was, so every now and then we jumped whenever one of us tripped or bumped into the other, or when we heard a broken branch sliding between the trees.

I jumped at a horrifying howl sandwiched in between two reverberating thunderclaps. It was something between a wail, a howl and a screech, with a bit of a crash and it sounded tortured and angry. We stopped and scanned between the trees. I drew my weapon and walked away. Drack stayed close to your mom while she took out her dagger, preparing for an upcoming attack.

After some time, maybe minutes, I came back, frowning and wary.

"There's some sort of animal across a small pond. It looks like a sphinx but it's smaller and it seems injured." I explained, "We might have to solve a riddle before we continue."

Before we got closer, Drack took a staff from his pack and assembled it.

"A portable staff!" I cried out.

"I know! Totally handy, right?" said Mom interrupting the story, excitedly. "I'm a witch but I had to learn to use swords and knives, because dragging my staff around was rather impractical. You have no idea how envious I was at the moment, especially because I've never seen that before. It isn't from our world, for sure, and it makes perfect sense on reflection."

So, we made our plan. I was to come out first to see if it really was a sphinx. If so, I'd signal them so we could all answer the riddle together, otherwise we'd have to fight. As it turned out, it was some sort of sphinx, just not the traditional kind you find in every other place. I couldn't tell whether it was a she or a he, so I will stick to an 'it'.

"Hello," I said. The sphinx was sitting and only looked at me before wailing again, apparently in sorrow.

"Are you guarding something?" I asked when it was silent.

The sphinx looked at me and sighed rather dramatically.

"I am supposed to be guarding this road" it answered, so I signaled and everyone came out cautiously. "But I see no point to it considering that no one has come here in over a month, ever since this damned storm began. And the rain makes me so depressed, I can't stop crying."

Your mom examined the sphinx while it cried and wailed.

"Are you really a sphinx?" she asked politely. "You don't talk like they usually do."

The sphinx sobbed and nodded, trying to calm down before it spoke.

"I know, I know! All the sphinxes talk in puzzles and rhymes." It complained. "I am a half sphinx, from my father's side. My mother was a banshee."

That explained its unsettling wails.

"Alright," continued your mom, "So here we are and we want to use the road. Usually sphinxes are released once their riddle is answered, right? So tell us your riddle and that way you can get out of this rain."

The half-sphinx seemed to brighten a little. Then it tried to stand and winced.

"What is it that ails my calf?" it asked.

After that, the half-sphinx kept sobbing and wailing, so we concluded that was its riddle. We stared at each other until your mom sighed and started to walk around the creature. She beckoned us to follow her and so we did.

The half-sphinx had part of a branch stuck on its right calf, near the hind leg, just like a huge splinter. We did all we could to take it out but it didn't move, so Drack sighed and motioned us to stay out of his way and, with a couple of words and a flash, the branch was out of the half-sphinx's calf.

Your mom took a look at the wound and used a minor spell to fix it before turning to talk to the half-sphinx.

"It was a branch you had stuck," she answered brightly. "Now it's gone and I have healed the worst part of it. Hopefully it will heal in a few days."

"Why, thank you!" it exclaimed relieved. "Now you shall pass. But before I leave, a warning: the warlock you are looking for is treacherous. Trust no one."

The creature smiled and left, eager to get out of the forest.

We kept on the road the creature had guarded. That night we didn't find any cave, so we had to sleep under the trees after making some sort of shelter with tree leaves and branches, as well as a ditch with stones to avoid being swept by the rain. We ate a cold dinner in silence and decided to keep a guard. The forest still didn't feel dangerous, but we had noticed that since taking the road, the trees seemed to be getting thicker.

"Let me guess," I interrupted again, already bored. "There were no monsters or animals during the night."

Dad's eye twitched a little but he just nodded and kept telling his story.

The forest became treacherous until we reached a huge swamp-like lake that seemed a pain to cross safely during the storm. We were feeling rather tired, so someone (I reckon it was your mother, but maybe not) proposed going to back to look for a different road. That was when we noticed that the path had closed on our backs and there was no way out, so we rearranged positions and continued slowly for the rest of the day.

Drack surprised us. We kept slipping and dragging our feet. Hell, I even lost my shoes to the mud at some point. Walking under the rain with muddy clothes was becoming old and tiring to us, but Drack seemed cheerful and clean. He even whistled to himself at some point.

Finally, we arrived in a clearing where there was a huge cave-like opening with a closed door. It was a simple round door made out of polished wood, with a doorknob in the middle giving no hint about whether it opened to the right or to the left.

We have talked about this for years, and both of us were expecting something like a castle, a cabin or a hut, not a cave, so it was rather disappointing, you know? But at that time we were so tired and bothered by the weather that we didn't care much about it.

We argued about staying in the clearing and trying to rest before going inside (just in case we had to fight), or just going inside and hope we didn't have to fight while being exhausted.

"I have the feeling you voted for going in right away" I said relieved. Finally the story was going somewhere! "I wouldn't have stayed in the rain, no matter what."

Mom chuckled.

"Yeah, that's exactly what I said at the moment." She said nodding. "I already felt uncomfortable in my dirty and soaked clothes, so I was rather desperate for a dry place."

Yes, even if it was impractical and reckless, like the adventure had promised, we reached the door and tried to open it.

But it didn't open.

Drack tried turning the doorknob while I pushed it rightwards, leftwards and downwards, and then while I pulled it, but it didn't move an inch either way.

Your mother tried picking the lock, but there was no lock.

I tried sticking a knife and carving out the doorknob, but since this was the entrance to a warlock's lair, of course it was protected against damage.

Drack tried to use some opening door spells, but they rebounded and ended burning a couple of trees.

Remembering some stories he had heard, Drack asked me to throw some light into the door in every possible angle while he searched for some inscription that had a clue about how to go in, but it didn't work either.

Your mother remembered yet another story about a door that required some blood as a toll payment in order to open, so she made all of us cut a finger and smear some blood on the door, and nothing happened.

We were angry and tired and hungry as well, so we despaired when the door didn't open, and that was the moment when your mom lost it.

"That's it, I can't take it no more!" she said while stomping towards the door. She reached the door and began kicking it, harder and louder with each word, while screaming.

"I... want... to... get... in... you... awful... door! I... hate... this... damned... storm... and... want... some... dry... clothes! Now... open... up... damn... you!"

We heard an earth splitting sound and some metal groaning and grinding before the door began opening. Drack's mouth hung open in surprise and he started shaking his head in disbelief, muttering something. I blinked and shrugged. We took our packs and walked inside, where your mom had already disappeared, seeming rather content with herself.

There was no corridor, for it was no cave. It was a huge one room house, with some plushy cushions on one side, a desk nearby, some bookshelves, a big squared table with more books and some eating utensils, a cooking spot, a huge fireplace with a blue and green fire that kept the whole place warm, and two doors, one of them already open.

Drack and I grabbed our weapons until we heard her whistling from the open door.

"This is a bathroom!" she shouted happily but rather disappointed. "By the way, there is no evidence of anyone living here in a while. Maybe the Silver Warlock went out on a trip?"

"Perhaps that's why the storm keeps going on." Drack ventured. "That way nobody can find this place and get inside while he's out."

I turned to look at Drack, who seemed strangely relieved. He was taking off his cape and hanging it behind the entrance door. I shrugged and did the same. Since we were there already, there was no point in going out into the storm, so we decided to have a warm dinner and rest before deciding what to do.

"And still, no fights whatsoever!" I felt tricked, the story seemed pointless. "I'm beginning to wonder whether the Silver Warlock actually existed, you know?"

"Please be patient," begged Dad trying to keep his calm. "We're almost finished."

Remember, Drack had hired us to bring him here, but we had also agreed that we would receive a reward and we hadn't taken a look into the place to see what we could pillage.

So, we went to sleep, warm and contented, but a bit disappointed because of the unexpected end of our adventure.

"But it wasn't the end!" I said eagerly.

"That's right, it wasn't." Dad smiled relieved. "And that's why you're here today."

Since it was clear the Silver Warlock had been away for some time, we made ourselves comfortable and slept. After a while, something woke me up. I looked around and found your mom already awake, but there was no sign of Drack. We heard a muffled noise coming from the second door, the one that we hadn't explored yet.

We looked carefully from behind the door frame and saw Drack mumbling to himself while he scanned and took things from the shelves, reading something, doing something on the floor and then putting the things back into the shelves. We got away from the door and whispered.

"He seems pretty sure of what he's doing back there" I remarked. She smacked me in the head, her face pale.

"Of course he's sure!" she whispered angrily. "Whatever it is, it has to be a powerful spell. And if he's finding things easily, it means he's been here before!"

I grimaced, understanding now the half-sphinx's words, for we had guarded the great Silver Warlock on his way back home. And we were fools for not realizing it before.

No, Chance, don't give me that look. I know you're thinking about why we didn't realize it sooner but, you see, since every one called him The Silver Warlock, his real name became forgotten: Dragon Vortis. We didn't get it because of his strange accent: when he introduced himself to us he didn't say "Drack Eon", he said "Drag-on". So yes, we were idiots.

Still, it was rather strange that he hadn't been able to get into his own place, so my curiosity won over my common sense and I decided to go into the room and ask him while your mother prepared to strike him.

He was scribbling in the center of the room with his back to the door, laughing quietly at some private joke, so I cleared my throat to make myself noticed. Dragon stood up and turned around, still smiling.

"That was a terrible idea!" I groaned. "And YOU reprimand me for being reckless?"

"We know it was reckless," agreed Mom, bothered. "But it's a hero's trait, just like youth."

Dad was already angry and cleared his throat, so everyone looked at him.

"Now shut it and listen to the rest of the story."

"Ah, you're awake!" exclaimed Dragon. "I was kind of expecting you to remain asleep for a few more hours."

"Yeah, I hoped so too," I said trying to sound nonchalant. "But somehow your moving around woke me up. What's all this?"

"Oh, it's just some spell I'm finishing." He answered coolly. "You see, I was working on this beauty when I went outside to get my last spell components, but that stupid door locked itself up and didn't let me in again, no matter what I did."

I racked my brain trying to think about a way to distract him away from the door so your mom could enter and attack him.

I couldn't think of anything, so I walked to the center of the room and tried to distract him while he kept talking.

"So, you were telling the truth when you said that the storm was cast to prevent anyone from coming into your place." I said nodding.

"That's right." He answered proudly. "If only I had kicked that damned door like your woman did, I would have saved me a month of trouble."

"But you didn't really need help getting here." I exclaimed. "Why hire us?"

Dragon laughed devilishly.

"Well, the final components for my spell are sphinx and banshee blood, and the last breath of a human before this death." He explained. "I was really lucky to find that halfling and trick it into guarding my lair. And now, I only need the last component!"

He cast a quick spell and knocked me out. When I opened my eyes, I was paralyzed and he had placed me in the center of the circle. Apparently he hadn't bothered to verify whether your mother had also woken up, but I didn't see her inside the room. Maybe she hadn't dared to get inside. If that was the case, then I still had a chance to stay alive. That was when Dragon laughed maliciously.

"She won't come to your rescue." He gloated. "I already cast a sleeping spell on her and I'll deal with her later."

He started chanting and my body began to shimmer inside the circle. I felt myself disappearing, Dragon's voice fading in the distance, and prepared for the inevitable. Then, suddenly everything stopped and I regained my hearing after a loud boom.

With my ears ringing, I looked around and saw your mom standing in the doorway with a perplexed expression on her face, eyes blinking rapidly, as if trying to fight sleep. On the floor all I could see was a grayish rag and a delicate miniature silver dragon figurine. I could move again, so I stood up and walked to get it. When I reached for it, I heard a strange argument.

"… not possible!" I heard someone say. I later recalled it was Dragon's voice but it echoed. It sounded… ethereal and distant. "But, how…?"

"Well, darling." A feminine voice said. She sounded angry, ethereal and distant too. "This is what happens when you use replacement ingredients for your spells. Now, your time for playing with humans is up."

"But... I was so close!" he cried out in despair.

"Now, now." The feminine voice seemed strained, as if she was losing her patience. "Let's go. Like it or not, you can't stay here anymore. Oh, and while we're leaving, I will dismiss your awful storm, this land doesn't take well to flooding."

When the voices faded I turned to help your mom, who could barely stay on her feet, and led her straight to the bed before I went to sleep too.

"And that's it," concluded Dad. "Oh, and the treasures we got were the portable staff and this place, with all the gold, weapons, spell books and so on, which helped us to become what we are now."

"I... can't believe it." I said rather disappointed. "That's all? That's how you vanquished him?"

"You have to admit that the official version sounds better than the way it really went," he protested. "Besides, no one would believe what really happened. We've had to make up part of the story to keep the people interested until we reach the end."

"Yup," Mom smiled knowingly. "When we got back to Silver Town we were ashamed of the truth, so we changed it. It does sound much better the other way, don't you think?"

I sighed heavily and nodded, exasperated

"You know what?" I said standing up, ready to leave. "You're right. I think the world doesn't actually need to know the truth."

Battle at Veldhaven
By Matthew Harvey

An overgrown moor is no fit place to camp, but that was exactly where we found ourselves; surrounded by thick, thick tangles of bracken, with wild grass and heather competing for free space. There was a mountain looming up in the distance, and out beyond that a threatening bank of murky cloud. In the middle of this unhappy wilderness in a partly threshed, partly stamped-down circle, three tents were crowded around a tiny fire.

That's where we started this particular little adventure. 'We' was me, Theng, a warrior in the heaviest plate dragons' teeth can buy and trying to get comfortable with a chill breeze finding every crevice in my armor.

The next face at the fire was our sorceress, officially titled as a 'third circle Arcane Initiate', even if she was too shy to call herself that. Tyriell looked freezing, robes wrapped tight under a blanket, and then under another blanket after that. It was a bitter evening with nothing to break the wind at that height but an occasional tall shrub.

Our third and final party member didn't seem to feel the cold at all. It was always hard to tell; Duen was a Questor of the Dwarven Stonefathers, and his unsmiling face could be chiselled from granite for all the expression he showed. He was wearing plate too. The Dwarven gods don't object to a priest wrapped in steel, and his armor made mine look delicate. He was also in charge of the map, and after a long scowl at the offending parchment he seemed to have come to a decision.

"We can either try and force a path down and into those woods," a pause while he indicated a mostly primordial forest down the slope of the mountain and stretching as far as we could see, "Or we can head around the northern side of the peak and camp down tomorrow in a village there, if it's still there."

"Sounds ominous," I said. Not that Duen was normally a ray of sunshine, but this was a little grim even for him. "We were warned there are orc bands all over these hills, and there's supposed to be a chieftain gathering them together a few at a time. A little village seems a likely target for that." Unfortunately, this made a lot of sense. The mountain orcs were one of the reasons we had been in the area, chasing a bounty a few weeks before.

Tyriell had gone pale by now. Not a great one for violent confrontation, our mage. She suggested a little timidly, "maybe we should head through the forest instead?"

Duen managed to hold off on a snapped response long enough for me to get there first. I admire Duen's strengths, but he is as delicate as a hammer in conversation. For all the power Tyriell could throw around, she was a quietly spoken one, and while I'm not the most gently spoken man I'm better at careful handling than the Dwarf. "If I remember the map right, we'd spend most of three weeks in the woods. That same ranger who warned us about the orcs said there were beasts in the forests that even the greenskins were scared of. The village seems a better option."

She nodded quietly, looking ashamed. As carefully as I always try to speak to her, I sometimes feel like a man kicking a puppy when she sinks into herself like that.

Before it became even more awkward, Duen moved us back on track. "Alright, it could as easily be the village has been left alone so far. That chieftain is supposed to be a smarter than average type, and the village is a fortified one. So we head there and stock up. The northern route around is a longer one, but like Theng said, the hazards are things we should be able to deal with."

Hazards like roving bands of unruly orcs or an entire army. I relished a good fight somewhere ahead and nodded confidently, while Tyriell merely accepted the obvious consensus with a quick bob.

A pot of stew had been slowly simmering over our little fire as we talked, and with a route planned we set to eating. The meal was filling and briefly I felt a little warmer, but all too quickly the heat was stolen by the lazy wind and we all chose to seek out our beds before we froze in our seats.

Dawn did not arrive quickly, or brightly. The overcast sky had closed in during the dark hours and brought a steady drizzling rain with it. Breakfast was a subdued affair not just because of the weather.

From the trees, we could hear the sounds of wildlife awakening as well. Not all the noises were recognizable ones; beyond the calls of birds were the roars and howls of bigger and more predatory things as well. Whether it was nerves or just her keener eyes, Tyriell swore there was something watching from the broken mess of the treeline. Neither Duen nor I were in a mood to debate the matter; the woods felt more alert than the busiest city I'd ever seen, and more vindictive than the most vicious mugger who had ever tried for my purse.

It was a miserable day of travel; the only real moment of pleasure to be had was when we came within sight of the intact walls of Veldhaven, the small village we were making for. Getting past the stout gates was no easy matter even then. From a platform within the wall, a stern and scarred man shouted down for us to stop. "We don't know you, strangers. We've no time for wandering nobodies, so make yourselves scarce."

I frowned at the cold dismissal but managed to take the lead in our response. "We're adventurers, circling Tor Cranneg towards the plains-cities. Open the gates and let us in, or I'll have to show you how we earned our license."

I took a step forward, a wary eye on the arrow head I could see following me over the wall. The man took a moment to look us over properly. Duen was belligerent and hulking on my left side, and Tyriell pale but standing tall by my shield arm. Then he grinned and offered a short bark of laughter. A wave of his hand and the gate swung ponderously open with two similarly grim men filling the gap.

"Alright then, adventurers. We'll not ask you to prove your grit today."

Beyond the cluster of men in rough leather at the gate, the village seemed almost deserted. Half the houses had the doors boarded and shutters drawn tight, and the few people we could see were trying too hard to walk by casually. Even Tyriell could tell these brave folk were scared for their lives; the threat posed by the rumored orc warlord made suddenly real and close. Between adventuring and time served in an army under siege, I could almost feel the future closing around us.

"We're going to have to fight to the death defending this place, aren't we?" I didn't bother making it a question, Fate just seems to follow that kind of path for adventurers.

Duen nodded, stern-faced as ever while Tyriell did her best to look brave. After exposure to me and especially our stony friend, she had gotten the hang of it well enough to fool most people. The local tavern keeper (of course we went to the tavern first, it's an old adventuring custom) wasn't most people, and picked up on her concerns in surprisingly kindly fashion.

"Young lady, I think you should be ready to move on as soon as you can. You look like far too nice a person to be caught up around here."

Duen and I were surprised at her response. Normally she'd nod and smile awkwardly or blush bright red, but she did neither. More forthright than I remember seeing, she answered, "Don't worry about me, sir. I can handle myself if I must."

It struck a chord somehow with the innkeeper, who gave a slow and approving smile as he gestured to his server. "Get some food in for these adventurers. A hot meal and chilled ale, I think?" Three eager nods answered the question and suddenly we were treated to much warmer expressions all round.

It turned out that timidity was poorly received in Veldhaven. The headman and his family had fled at the first murmur of orcs, and sparked a flood of people out of the gates. Tyriell, meek as she looked, had enough steel in her spine to buy us some quick respect and we didn't waste it.

With an afternoon free and a fight in the wind, Duen and I did what all sensible campaigners do and visited the smith. It wasn't a great surprise to find he had little fresh gear available but neither the dwarf nor I were buying anyway.

Duen, resplendent in his mountain-forged plate, was an immediate success, and while the smith worked out a few little dents from my armor I managed to make a positive impression of my own. I mentioned a military career in passing, but I was apprenticed as a smith before I found my real joy in battle. Leveling the heat of his forge and helping to put a rough edge to his ready sword blanks, I teased out a little more on the local situation. A blacksmith will gossip with his fellows more cheaply than a tavern keeper will, knowledge I rarely waste.

The orc causing all the trouble was called Vok'Gorroth, a priest of the orcish god of blood and battle. As a disciple of a war god, it was no great shock he was a strong warrior in his own right. Rumour said he had slain three warchiefs to bring their clans into his growing army, and more had flocked to him after that. A handful of smaller clans now followed his banner, and one of the larger had been soundly defeated and absorbed in a brutally cold winter of bloodshed. The Shattered Tooth clan, one of his early conquests, was apparently prowling the local area and preparing to strike at the village.

Whatever else I could say of him, Duen was a pragmatist and blunt as a hammer. He wasted no time in informing the smith that we would likely be moving on before any such attack came and I felt the mood change at once. The man's face hardened and with a few more sharp blows he declared gruffly our equipment was as good as his skill could manage. We were, he said, free to leave his forge.

Feeling cold creep out in our wake, I knew our stay would become a lot less pleasant in the face of Duen's declaration. The change in the smith's demeanor cut me like a knife; I could also hear him name me a coward as we walked away.

"Duen, what were you thinking? These people obviously don't care for cowards, and you all but told them we plan to run away."

For his part, Duen held a firmer grip on his temper. "We don't have time to stop at every little hamlet and solve the ills of the world. I'm no coward as you well know, but sitting under siege from a mob of bloody-minded greenskin murderers is not a good use of our time."

I couldn't fault the statement. Four months trapped in a city under siege years before had shown me how bad it could be, and I'd no desire to feel that numbing misery again. But I have never backed down from a fight I could win, and I was marshaling arguments to keep us here on the long walk back to the inn. But of all people, it was the quiet Tyriell who set her foot down. When Duen informed her quietly that we'd not be staying around for a fight, she blurted out her disagreement.

"No, Duen. We can't leave yet. I Saw it."

We stared at her for a second and she flushed red before explaining more quietly. "Last week, when we defeated that orcish bandit, I had a vision. And in the vision, there was an orc, a huge brute, with the mountain hanging behind him. He was killing people Duen, on all sides. Then I saw our sign, the one we seal contracts with?"

She looked at us, to be sure we'd understood and we nodded recognition. As an authorised adventuring group we had a registered seal as well, stamped on every contract we accepted. "It was on a banner, and then the orc's banner was there too, an angry face with a shattered tooth."

Duen and I shared a look as she continued. The reference was blindingly obvious and he couldn't help but look annoyed that Fate was stepping on his plan. "The banners clashed, and there was a flash of lightning, and then blood. One banner was still standing, but I couldn't see whose it was. Then I woke up, and that was all."

She sat quietly staring at her drink until finally Duen sighed in defeat.

"You don't often See things missy, but you've not been wrong yet. If we're fate bound to cross paths with the green stain, so be it." I sat back with a grin and the Dwarf offered a faint grimace. I couldn't help but tease, even if it had been an act of the gods that kept us there. "I told you we'd be fighting here, Duen. And woe betide the orcs who cross our path."

The tavern keeper had approached while Tyriell had been speaking, the grim look on his face going through mystified to enlightened as it became clear that Duen's declaration had been made in haste. He turned away without speaking, whatever he had been planning to say obviously unimportant now that we were planning on staying for a little while.

Only half the story had spread by evening, when conflicting mutterings did the rounds of the quiet tavern until I finally grew tired of being called a coward behind my back. Odd as it might sound for a warrior to admit, I sometimes have a shamefully short grip on my temper. I stood and rapped my tankard until I had attention; needless, as every eye was on me anyway. "We'll be going nowhere until these broken-face orcs are dead and un-mourned. And any man who wants to question my skill or my nerve can step forward now, and fall down spitting teeth." There was a moment of quiet; it was a common occurrence following one of my tavern speeches as the locals waited for the inevitable responder.

Sure enough, one of the larger and drunker men hauled himself to his feet and declared with a slur "I'll knock your face in, coward, and dance on your grave when the orcs kill you a day's ride away."

A space cleared in an instant, and with a dangerous grin I stepped into the gap and took up a fighting stance. The big man knew what he was about, but between drink and my own experience he didn't stand a real chance. His punches were strong but well telegraphed, leaving me easily able to block them. Bad temper hurt me more as I battered at his face, rocking him on his heels and as I had threatened spilling two of his teeth. He collapsed seconds later, senseless, and I was left feeling a little foolish over my outburst and nursing a freshly broken knuckle besides.

The crowd gave a little cheer and a scattering of applause and the bartender brought over a new drink, but no more comment was made on the scrappy fight or the comments that had caused it. They did at least stop after that.

With so much talk of an orcish attack, I was surprised to sleep the night through. But it was the dawn watch that called an alarm, and by the time we'd gotten armored and ready for a fight the rest of the village was ready as well. Leather vests, spears and shields seemed to have materialized all round, with war bows in some peoples' hands besides.

Over the wall, it seemed that the shattered tooth clan had assembled en masse. The clan wasn't the largest armed force I'd ever seen; I'd marched to war before and seen armies that could flood a valley with warm bodies. Still, two hundred or more orcs were gathered in all their feral glory against the forty or so defenders. Against the walls and bows within Veldhaven, I could see orcs with shoulder bags of javelins, and a few in rough looking iron plates clustered around a crude ram. Experience told me that even the least armored body before us would take a deal of killing, and the gates would only hold them for so long.

The worst of it was the orc at the head of the coming attack. Tyriell's description had entirely failed to prepare me for the sight of him, and from a quiet curse at my shoulder it had taken Duen aback as well. More than seven feet tall and wearing blackened iron plate, 'huge brute' seemed too weak. Heavy scars marked his face, cutting across one eye which was miraculously undamaged and through the line of his mouth. A ruined tusk jutted beneath a gristly mess of scar tissue there, obviously the source of his clan name.

He was within range of the bows on the wall, but his sheer presence kept us from taking a shot. Swaggering forward, he advanced another few paces and drew breath for a speech. Before he could begin he shifted his footing and whipped a heavy vambrace in front of his eyes, which suddenly grew an arrow as someone finally gathered their nerve.

He laughed, a deep rolling sound filled with deadly good humor at the attempt on his life. "Good try, little men. But you are feeble before Gach'ak of the Shattered Tooth. I will remember your deaths today and laugh, even as I tear the meat from your bones at my feasting!"

Never one to leave an enemy with the last word I was preparing to reply when Duen bellowed at the greenskin in a voice rough with anger. "Gach'ak of the bloodied lip, step forwards and die in the dust! Today you will taste my hatred, and the hatred of a thousand of my kin, when I cast your spirit into the dark wastes of the next world!"

I had rarely heard such a threat from my friend, but recalled he bore a particular hatred for the flesh eating practices of certai barbaric clans. Abhorrent to all right-thinking folk, I knew that Duen had more cause to be angered than most. Several of his own bloodkin had been killed and devoured in such a fashion, and there was a sworn oath made by all his family to see those monsters dead.

Clearly, the orc warchief before us had never had such a response as he roared his anger, beating a hefty club against the ground as his followers joined the shout. It cowed the defenders as the orcs began building to frenzy and I knew it would be disastrous if we let it continue much longer. I had borrowed a bow, and as I drew for my first shot I shouted out a quick order to spur the villagers to action.

"Archers, if you value your lives you'll loose until your hands won't grip! Nock and fire, and don't let up!"

I matched action to words and was pleased to see my first arrow joined by others from the wall. It was equally disappointing to see the lack of effect it had on the orcs hammering and shouting before us.

The volley startled them, moving the gathered clan to action as a second round of arrows flew. This one was more effective, and a few orcs in the front line dropped with two or three arrows in them. At my side, Duen was in prayer, calling on his ancestors and his gods to strengthen his arm and his allies.

Along the line, I could see the stirring of air and first glowing signs of a spell forming from Tyriell's arcane utterances.

A sharp-eyed orc amongst the masses had seen the same thing and took steps to counter it at once. At a yell, spears flew toward Tyriell, caught up in her casting. Before I could call a warning, one of the villagers had stepped forward, placing himself and his shield in the way of the throws. I gaped, losing the flow of my archery at the sight of the javelins smashing through the shield and one tearing into the meat of the arm braced against it. I had seen spears thrown in war but never cause so much damage.

The man staggered, white-faced in shock within seconds but he had bought Tyriell valuable time. Dark hair billowing and with bluewhite fire gathered about her hands, she cast a bright beam at the front ranks of orcs. It leapt and coiled, consuming those struck in a halo of flame. A dozen or more orcs in a single strike, but she sagged, obviously feeling the strain of the powerful spell. She didn't stop though, gathering in the fire for a second dancing blast of energy.

More orcs fell, but the clear danger she posed was not lost on Gach'ak. There was an answering hail of javelins, and this time one passed between the warding shields and pierced her thin robes. A wash of blood darkened the cloth and with a gasp she collapsed, the fire and twisting wind dying away in an instant. Eagle-eyed villagers scooped her out from under the feet of the archers and back toward the tavern and the healer.

With rage building in my own heart, I fired again and again, then abandoned my bow as the armored orcs crashed against the gate.

Between the weight of their ram and the bulk of their own bodies, they shattered the panels, slowed but by no means stopped by the heavy timbers. The towering shape of Gach'ak was at the forefront of the orcs rushing in their wake, still bellowing in rage and with foam drooling from his damaged lips. Hot blood surging, I threw myself off the firing step with axe and shield in hand and began carving into the mob. The villagers straggling line wouldn't hold forever, but for a few glorious moments we stopped their charge.

Then a great roar came from the front of the green mob and I saw one of the village militia soar backwards with blood spraying from a terrible wound in his chest. Another man was rushing to fill the gap, but Duen was already stepping forward with his mace swinging.

Over the hammer of metal on metal and the cries of the wounded, I could hear him shouting, a prayer to the Stonefathers. A bright flash of light that I recognized from previous battles was followed by a guttural scream.

Semi-molten metal plates span away from the ruin Duen had made; one less of the armored orcs to worry about. For a few moments, I lost track of my friend and the huge chieftain while I tangled with spear and club wielding barbarians in the shield line. To my left, two men staggered backwards, one sagging to his knees and collapsing as Gach'ak emerged through the breach. Three more of his heavy guard followed him and our thin defenses looked in danger of folding back and being overrun.

The battle-sound was ringing in my head, thus I followed the only thought I could grasp. With the same war-cry my ancestors had given, I smashed back the orc before me and broke from the line myself, bellowing a challenge at the frothing monster. One of his guards stepped in first and took three hard blows before he fell, oozing blood from rents in his crude plate. I barely caught a strike on my shield and staggered backwards as the chieftain himself stepped in. One of the other brutes stepped forward, then halted at an unintelligible roar from his leader. It seemed this was to be a one on one fight for now.

With the destructive presence of Gach'ak in check, the stalwarts of the town guard rallied for a few moments and re-formed solid defensive rings. We were still terribly outnumbered, and with the wall breached we looked likely to make a heroic last stand at best.

Mine seemed destined to come first; for all the weight of armor I had, however hard I braced my shield his blows were punishing me, and my own seemed frustratingly poor. In the pauses while he drew back for another crushing blow, I could see where his badly-made armor was buckled and split from my axe but the flesh beneath was whole.

My own plate was by now gouged and scarred and my shield all but ruined, though none of my blood stained the ground.

A sudden shift in his fighting stance caught me off guard and a low blow smashed into my hip, tossing me to the ground. He stamped down, pinning my shield arm and leaving me staring up into mad red eyes. He grinned, slaver speckling his jaw and raised his iron-bound club to finish me. I refused to close my eyes or look away, intending to go into the next world as bravely as I knew how.

His club didn't fall, at least on me. While I had battled to defend myself, Duen had fought free of the melee and started looking for the biggest trouble. Another of the armored orcs had fallen before him while I was struggling, and his intervention came just as I was about to die there on the ground. His mace once more aglow, he barreled into the burly orcs midriff at a full run.

More than three hundred pounds all told, he rocked Gach'ak back on his heels and drew a grunt of pain as the chieftains' orc-made breastplate creased under the sudden load.

"Ancestors guide my blows! Strike down this foul monster!" Duen's shout was followed by a Dwarven one and in the light shed by his weapon I could see something retreat from around the orc.

The blow could be no harder than my own had been but this one left a greater mark than all mine combined. Gach'ak staggered and roared in pain and confusion, clutching at one flank for a second before madness rose in his eyes again and he waded forward, swinging great haymaking blows at the Dwarf. Duen had opened a breathing space for me, but before the bellowing juggernaut even my stalwart companion was being driven back. Like me, he found himself warding off battering blows and staggering before impacts that would shatter bone.

But I had gathered myself now, and with the Shattered Tooth's warding broken my axe's edge was proven keen. I leapt to Duen's aid as he had to mine, setting Gach'ak reeling with a braced rush with my broken shield and a punishing overhand strike that split the collar of his armor and left the damaged breastplate hanging loose.

Seeing their chieftain in trouble, the orcs' discipline began to falter. Some broke from the brawls around the villages last defenders and raced to reinforce their leader while others stepped clear, discouraged. Still others flew into a true battle rage and began flailing about them, a threat to friend and foe.

Those who broke towards us were scattered as Duen barreled through them, cast aside as Gach'ak roared and howled like a beast, driven beyond reason by pain and our determined resistance. Casting aside his club, he lunged at me, grappling for my throat. Abandoning my broken shield at last, I left my axe to hang from its loop and desperately tried to fend the monster off.

In his fury, he proved the stronger and forced me to the ground again to begin choking the life from me. At the edge of my vision, I could see Duen on his feet again, surrounded by howling orcs and fighting for his life. Beyond that I could see the clusters of militia struggling with more of the greenskins, discipline gone and fatigue dragging on every movement.

I was on the verge of blacking out when a crash of thunder broke over me. Blue-white light blinded me for precious seconds as I struggled at the weight bearing down on me. Then it occurred to me; there was no weight on my chest now. No hands clutched at my throat and no red eyes burned above me. I rolled onto my side, dragging in breathes like a leaking bellows and looked around in amazement. Fifteen feet away, the smoldering shape of the huge orc groaned and pawed at the dirt. I could see Duen on the ground, sparks curling and dancing on his armor as he twitched and cursed.

Of the few defenders and their assailants, I was hard pressed for a few seconds to tell between them. They had been smashed from their feet en masse, many bearing scorch marks and none with any fight left in them.

Gach'ak alone seemed defiant, forcing himself to one knee and trying to stand despite the incredible punishment he had taken. I dragged myself upright, feeling every blow I had taken all over again and aching in every muscle.

Axe in hand, I stepped forward ready to continue the fight but he was beyond his limit now and didn't regain his feet.

The massive orc grinned at me through his burns with bloody foam pink on his lips.

"Vok'Gorroth will still take this place. Make your peace little warrior, and cherish your remaining days. Your soul will feed our god soon."

I shook my head at his final words and raised my axe for the last blow. "When you face your god, tell him the Silver Trinity isn't done with his servants."

My strike chopped deep into the orc's neck, almost severing it and spraying me in gore. I swear, in his last second he turned to give me a clearer shot. Frowning and with the chieftain's blood running down my face, I turned to examine the wreckage left from the battle.

While I had been distracted many of the remaining orcs, those able, had gathered their wits and taken to their heels. Few of Veldhaven's own had lived through the bloody battle, a bare dozen on their feet and already moving to find their wounded. Duen was walking with them, but where the villagers were gathering up their own, he was about the grim business of finishing the crippled orcs abandoned by their fleeing comrades.

The source of the lightning eluded me at first, until I spied the village healer struggling with a shape a dozen yards beyond the edge of the carnage.

Forcing weary limbs into a run, I clattered over and knelt at the woman's side, carefully taking the weight of her burden. Pale-faced, Tyriell looked up to me and murmured a near-silent question. I couldn't hear her, but there was only one thing she could have wanted to know. I offered her a smile made gruesome by my bloody face paint and offered the answer I knew she wanted. "Yes Initiate, we won."

She gave a weak return smile and I saw her eyelids flutter, then her head sagged back against my arm. I almost panicked, until a glance at the healer showed her counting my friend's heartbeats.

"Into the inn with her, warrior. She'll live to fight another day if we've anything to say about it."

Duen and I spent all that morning worrying over our shy friend. We spent our nervous energy in dragging the orc carcasses clear of the gate and helping with the honorable dead of the village. More than half the defenders were gone;

those who had fallen had not lived long within the pitiless melee and all the survivors were wounded.

As we waited on Tyriell's recovery, the smith sought us out. "My thanks to you both. We'd have been dead but for you and your friend. If I might, I'd like to ask a favor." He looked awkward, almost ashamed, and I shared a puzzled glance with my comrade.

"Ask away. There's a hell of a mess to clear here, and no sense waiting."

The man coughed and looked around. "We'll not be staying long enough to clear this. There's not even a dozen men can fight right now, and barely more than that if we all heal up clean. We're quitting the village. I was hoping you two and your mage friend would head out with us?"

We shared a second glance and a decisive nod from Duen sealed the matter. "As soon as Tyriell is fit to travel, we'll be glad of the company. Speaking of the brave lass, best be seeing how she feels, eh?"

As it turned out, she was awake again, though weak as a kitten.

The appreciative murmurs from the men she'd saved seemed to be mortifying for her; she was flushed bright red and half-hidden beneath a sheet when we approached. She wasted no time in asking "can we leave soon? Everyone keeps staring at me, and they won't stop saying thank you."

Even Duen managed a smile, while I chuckled at her embarrassment. "We'll leave once you're able to walk, but we'll be traveling along with these folk while they go down to the city. This attack took everything we could throw at it and we barely held on.

The greenskins will be back, but we'll not be here to wait on them this time. And Tyriell?" "Hmm?" "Thank you for saving us. You're a treasure."

And for once, she didn't hide from the compliment.

Silver Horn
By Ricardo Victoria

During those times lost in the mists of the ancient legends of incongruent events, there was a folk tale about a journey of certain legendary status. Now, these kind of stories are a well-known set-up for inspirational tales about courage, friendship and heroism. But, those only work if the heroes portrayed are charismatic and ooze epicness with a single glance. Those kind of heroes were the shiny beacons of hope for despairing lands. And telling a story like that would be fine. Of those, there are plenty and they are more expensive and expansive.

But not this time, not in this case. While this is a story about a journey involving a mystic item (another cursory element in such tales), the heroes are hardly charismatic and far from being paragons of anything. The only shiny thing coming from them were their false, golden teeth. If you met any of them in a bright alley, you would run away. Because for every epic hero with good public relations, there is also a poorer, run-down version, equally worthy of praise, but not as marketable (so no movie deals for these folks, centuries later when their stories were rediscovered).

Fraog was one these run-down folks on a mission. He had scruffy hair, languid features and a disproportionately tall height for a regular 18-year-old who wore tattered clothes and worn leather boots. His face was full of freckles and he had a few crooked teeth.

In fact, the only sign of having a quality beyond the rest of his peers was his bright green eyes that gave him an eerie, almost feylike visage during the nights. He had been living at the monastery since he was a newborn after his mother passed away in a cruel winter outside the nearby village, her origin or name unknown. He got his name from a dog-tag tied to his tiny hands (now hanging from his neck) that the monks suspected, were from his father, though the name wasn't recognized in the region by anyone. It was almost as if he just appeared one day next to a dead body, like those old nursery rhymes that talked about lost princes. However, one thing was sure: Fraog wasn't a lost prince, because he could sleep soundly, no matter how many peas were placed under his bed.

On his eighteenth birthday, instead of receiving a gift that marked his inclusion into the not-so-responsible adult world, he got a mission. He had been tasked by the Archpriest of the monastery where he was an inmate, as many orphan often were, to carry the neither-so-fabled nor well-known Silver Horn to That Place, located deep into the Humbagoos rainforest, before the next lunar eclipse.

Fraog was chosen because everybody in the monastery and the nearby village knew he wasn't going to fail. And they were so sure because he was more stubborn than a mule with authority issues. That was the main reason behind the Archpriest's decision to send Fraog... well, that and the barely mentioned fact that he was eating too much food, especially the abbot's favorite chocolate dessert and needed an excuse to get rid of him, and while the mission was really important, the abbot was a lazy man that preferred to spend his time reading magazines instead of you know, carrying (out) the Archpriest's mission.

In all honesty, Fraog didn't have any remarkable magical ability and he was a lousy warrior to be fair. But his stubbornness reached level of mythic proportions, to the point that his own body refused to acknowledge any injury so it simply healed it as fast as it happened.

Fraog was surrounded by his own legends among his peers because of this. For example, the other orphans used to scare each other telling the tale of their older 'brother' who once grew back his left pinky finger that he cut off while practicing with a rusty sword as if he were a legendary warrior of the ancient times. In hindsight, his ability was certainly useful, since the road to the rainforest was plagued with dangers, wastelands, evil towns of inbreed mutants, cannibal deli restaurants and every single non-touristic spot any travel guide worth two copper pieces could imagine (as no sane travel writer would actually go there and verify the entry cost to the local attractions).

Other than that, Fraog was a simple boy with simple dreams: travel around, meet a lovely girl of the sorcerous kind, have a lot of sex and a couple of kids and a castle, you know, the whole Grenadian Dream often dreamt by boys in monasteries.

Fraog had been traveling for several weeks now, as he lost his transport early on when he traded his donkey for a bag of magical potatoes that had the properties of always pointing to the place you didn't want to go in first place and of looking like the faces of a popular folk band of itinerant bards. Not very useful indeed, but Fraog, although a good person, was as naïve as they come and the donkey ended in the hands of a poor married couple that were trying to get to some old farm where the wife would give birth to a legendary once and future king as prophesized. But that is other story and you paid only for this one.

During his travel, Fraog had already survived encounters with a couple of lost furry green orcs trying to reach their village, a short-sighted dragon hoarding a treasure made of comedy books and at least three full regiments of mosquitoes and assorted killer bugs that got bored of trying to draw blood from Fraog's thick skin. Then he crossed the speeding currents of the Myrdiac River by wading through it one stubborn step at a time. By the time he reached the far side of the bank, he was a hundred miles downstream.

Certainly, he was not the classic prototype of hero, with square jaws and muscles upon muscles upon muscles that made him look like a walking mountain with the aura of a king. And it was even more certain that he wasn't material for monk, unless you were trying for the kind of pesky monks living in a secluded monastery upon a mysterious mountain developing ancient techniques to shoot fireworks from their hands, pretty handy for parties and festivals.

But Fraog was closer to the hero type than the monk. He had this aura around him that made the other kids back at orphan house call him 'pissed by fat'. Though I'm pretty sure the translator got that last line wrong.

After a couple of days of non-stop walking and not so much amusement beyond a few trinket sellers and intelligent mosquitoes developing a drill to allow them suck his blood, Fraog decided that a particular spot at a forest near a bridge and a river was the perfect place to take a rest. He took seat on a greenish stone, close to the river and took out his water bottle to fill it with not-so-fresh fresh water. He was planning to give a look at the old, blurry map that worked as guide for him and to see where he was going.

According to his calculations –because despite appearances he wasn't dumb, just not very educated - he was a couple of miles from his finish line.

After drinking water and putting the map back in his duffel bag, he took a few minutes to admire the Horn again.

It was still a mystery why he had to take a horn, no matter how pretty and shiny it was, to a Specific Place before Certain Date, but he gave it a deep thought. He remembered that when he was a kid, the old people at the village told ancient legends about it, the reasons why it was decorated with silver branches of the ancient goddess of hunt and war. No one mentioned how the Horn ended in that poor village, nor why it had to be returned to its place now and not before, but then again neither the monks nor the villagers were very honest to begin with, which made Fraog wonder if piousness was a sickness rather than a desired quality for them, since they avoided it with force, but then again, these were the ways of such tales.

Rumors about how the Horn could summon the most astonishing creatures, such as the fabled Montoc Dragons to support their master in combat and how the Moonriders of old used it for some raids on the dark tribes that worshiped the Shadow King from Outside Reality. Then again, those old people believed that the Moon was made of bland cherry pie and that the riverside where he used to play was the place where pirates with metallic arms have buried a treasure, a bag where at the end the only content was a series of green chips with golden lines in intricate circuits that barely worked as coasters.

He was aware of what would happen if the Horn did not arrive in time, he wasn't going to achieve his dreams if the world was going to end because you arrived late to a mystical appointment, which was the warning that the monks had given him. Otherwise, the Silver Horn could unleash the sealed power contained in it, which was something the world do not wanted to witness again; just ask what's left of the Kingdom of Umo, which is now a lovely, brand new beach with melted stones peppering it here and there. So there was extra motivation for Fraog to carry out the mission, because dreams can't be built upon smoking ashes.

Regardless, curiosity struck again like a wasp stings you in the most inconvenient time and Fraog took the horn towards his mouth to blow it. Luckily for those betting the safety of the world on such a lumbering kid, the rock... well rocked, making him fall square in on his face into the muddy earth. When he managed to stand, he saw a tall, greenish troll gazing at him with intensity, while rubbing his back.

With a deep, angry voice he said: "Give me a reason to not eat you as punishment for sitting on my poor and pained back."

"It is your fault. Why the hell did you have to lie in the middle of the road and look like a rock?" was Fraog's reply, with a brave gaze while unsheathing his rusty sword, which made a clanking noise just from being out.

"You are nothing more than a piece of insolent meat, which I will devour with pleasure and a nice cup of warm apple wine. But before that, I would like to know your name."

"What for?"

"So I will know what name I should write in your resting plot."

"A most reasonable reason indeed. My name is Fraog Unvil Tessla."

"Tessla? Are you the son of my good old friend Colin Unvil Tessla, legendary hitchhiker who traveled the Gereno River in a poorly made raft and eradicated hundreds of cannibal tribes with an infection of Lamporrea?"

Fraog was surprised at such description that let him know more about his father, although he wasn't as thrilled to hear about his hygiene habits.

"I guess, the only thing I have from my father are his dog tags. And while I desire to know more about him I have to leave. I have a Very Important Mission to fulfill."

"Of course not. Now instead of eating you, I will split your head in two first. Then I will cook you."

"And to what do I owe such honors?"

"Your father owed me a lot of money, therefore, you are dreaming if you think I will let you go so easy."

"Hey listen, I'm kinda in a hurry, as I need to get to that Specific Place in the Humbagoos' jungle before the moon sets and I'm running out of time. Would you consider joining me in my mission and once we finish it, then you can consider eating me or splitting my skull in two? That way you can keep me always in sight and I get to hear more about my father before meeting him in the Great Halls of Drunkenness and 24-hour Divine Eatery."

"A most reasonable request. Let's go then."

The sun started to set on the horizon and as both travelers walked down the remaining road, while discussing the merits of being eaten or crushed and what kind of spices go better with humanoid flesh.

They also discussed the latest rumors of the approaching war from the dark riders of the eastern steppes and other dealings that were barely the interest of vagabonds and other lowly beings.

The troll, which by the way was named Dagodet and was actually a gourmet, lectured Fraog on his travails with the latter's father, apparently one of the most renowned vagabonds in these parts of the world, allowing him to know more of his ancestry, but that is way too much detail to go here in this tale and it will take us into a lengthy detour of five books.

Quickly, perhaps due the entertaining chat, they reached the Humbagoos' jungle and crossed it in record time – maybe because most dangerous creatures were already scared of Dagodet - and reached the Specific Place just in time. Sadly, they missed the obvious fact that they were being followed by a most unsavory troupe.

At the center of the Specific Place was a monolith of grey limestone with engravings of runes from forgotten languages and images referring to the moon, the mysterious Moonriders, riding strange winged creatures that exhaled will-o'-the-wisp from their nostrils and engaged in epic battles.

Of course, Fraog and Dagodet imagined all of the above because one of them actually spoke the forgotten languages engraved in the Monolith. Anyways, Fraog was going to put the Silver Horn into the slot dedicated for it, when a horde of skeletal figures, probably zombies or poorly paid soldiers jumped on the vagabonds and started to attack.

The problem was that the horde members were not particularly effective nor dangerous, as they were lousy attackers and as we established before, Fraog's body simply denied the existence of any injury and Dagodet, being a troll, well... he was a troll and those are usually pretty hard to hurt. It is easier for them to damage a vertebral disc by lifting their mothers-in-law – yes they have several, trolls are polygamous – to actually take them down, even using magic and even more if the troll in question is intelligent. And Dagodet was a pretty smart one, besides being a gourmet. No, the actual issue with these enemies was that they were too many and also, they stunk like rotten meat.

The two unusual partners managed to take down a great quantity of them, but that didn't matter because the leader of the troupe finally made his big appearance – dramatic lightning and thunder included. With a classically trained evil laugh, this darkly dressed short man walked towards Fraog and Dagodet. Lifting his finger towards the Silver Horn, he yelled with a scrappy voice:

"You fool! Do you think to leave a masterpiece of arcane magic so it can rot with the ages? You have no idea of what it is capable of in the right hands. You will be serving the Horn's purpose better by giving it to me."

"What are you talking about?" Fraog asked, really annoyed at the deranged speech. As you can see, he would also have little patience for modern politicians.

"That is the Legendary Silver Horn, gifted by the Moon Goddess to old raiders of the gibed moon clan so they could summon the Faiths, the mystical creatures made for epic combat!"

Fraog gave a good look to the Horn, which was reflecting the light of the moon before being covered by the eclipse.

"Give me that Horn and I might spare your pitiful life." The short warlock said to Fraog.

"Are you kidding? I have a mission and I shall fulfill it no matter what." Fraog replied in epic hero voice. Even he was surprised to hear it.

"Such stubbornness, proper of a mule. Ok, let's make a deal: If you give me the Horn, I will not only spare your life, but I will give you a job as my main mercenary. Otherwise my troupe will tear you limb by limb."

Fraog gave the Horn a last look and with the moon almost fully covered by the eclipse, he looked to the Monolith. The warlock divined his reaction and rallied his zombies to attack. Fraog was tempted to blow the Horn, but reminded himself of the warning that the monks gave him and his mission. This time it wasn't his stubbornness or fate, but his sense of duty stopping him, as he made a mad dash towards the Monolith to put the Horn in its resting place.

He managed to fend off the zombies and was close to putting the Horn in place just in time when the desperate warlock threw a purple fireball to kill Fraog Luckily for our not-so-special hero, Dagodet interrupted the attack by using his body as shield.

"Do what you have to do. I will deal with the puny human," Dagodet said with grave voice, while walking menacingly towards the warlock.

The short enemy, desperate, threw several fireballs towards Dagodet, setting his shoulders aflame. However, the troll advanced and, without a flinch, broke the warlock's neck, throwing him far away into the jungle. Just in that moment, Fraog set the Horn into in its proper place and a bright light emanated from the Monolith, ending the eclipse sooner than expected. The shiny light destroyed the zombies and from it, the ghostly visage of a warrior walked towards Fraog. With a supernatural—but melodic voice—the ghost said: "Thank you mortal for returning what was ours. For avoiding the temptation of blowing it and not allowing evil hands to lay a touch upon it. For your iron will. For this, the Moon Goddess has deemed you fit for two rewards, one being now the McCool name which your descendants will bear and the other..."

With that, the ghost disappeared and along with it, the Silver Horn, leaving the place empty sans Fraog and Dagodet. The night was now clear and peaceful.

"What a shame the ghost didn't tell you the second reward and only left you with a lousy title." Dagodet said while dusting the ashes from his body. Fraog turned his head to face his peculiar partner, with a mix of happiness and amazement.

"You are safe! I thought that by now you would be dust and ashes. Why did you help me? Not that I'm not grateful."

"First, you need more than purple fireballs to take down an old troll. Second, I helped you because you are the son of a dearest friend."

"And yet you are planning to split my skull."

"Well, a debt is a debt."

"Do you mind if we discuss it with a beer in the next town? All this fighting left me hungry and thirsty," Fraog replied while sheathing his rusty sword and hitting the road.

"Fair enough, but you pay."

"I'm afraid to say, but there wasn't any monetary reward. The only valuable thing was the Horn and now it is gone. So with what do you propose I will pay?"

"That is how your dad got his debt."

Both vagabonds keep discussing the point with happy voices, following the road towards the Next Village. The night fell upon the Humbagoos' Jungle, while a shining falling star crossed the sky, like a sign of the things to come for all.

The End?

A Taste For Battle
By Leo McBride

No matter how many times he thought it through, Weasel still couldn't fathom how he'd gotten here.

Here he stood, in the beggar end of a rat canyon with a Reaver warband on the way to kill him for the simple reason that he stood between them and a pox-ridden village he could care less for.

Weasel spat and paced up and down again, despising the sun for edging noon and making his drink-addled head pound again.

He'd like to blame the drink, but he hadn't supped enough mead to agree to walk into certain death – just enough to turn the serving girl he'd bedded into a sultry princess from distant

Camarr. That had worked, as he'd convinced her of his heroism with outlandish tales of his daring adventures – at least one of which had actually been about him.

Yet, somehow, he was tumbled out of bed this morning by the villagers who splashed his head into water a few times before reminding him (as if he'd ever known in the first place) of his pledge to defend the village from the oncoming warband.

Somehow, his objections slipped away from his lips as the stable boy helped him don his armor with all the expertise you might expect from someone who only ever handled horses and not people – the bindings still chafed – and finally he stood here, in Hook Canyon, the place where he'd die. Which reminded him. Stood here. In these boots. By the gods, these were new boots and he'd do his damnedest to walk that squeak out before he died. He started pacing again.

"You'll wear a groove," said Rasten from where he stood, leaning casually against the sheer rock wall of the narrow canyon.

"Hmph, you can shut up too. My head is killing me," snapped Weasel.

Rasten smiled, leaning back and stretching his tall, muscular frame.

"Well," he said, "that'll save the Reavers the trouble."

"Oh very funny," Weasel snarled, "You know, you could have said something, anything, to get us out of this."

"Aye," Rasten nodded. "Aye? Aye? We're talking about the prospect of you saying just a few words that would mean the difference between you and me moving on to Port Elista and the finest whorehouse on the Thunder Coast or standing here waiting to die on a day with altogether too much sun and all you can say is aye? Aye? Why didn't you say anything?"

Rasten bent down and picked up the carefully-wrapped bundle he had brought with him from the village and paused to look up at the sun before answering.

"It seemed like a good plan," he said after due consideration.

Weasel sputtered. "Plan? What plan?"

"The one you came up with last night. The one you told Esme."

Weasel's earlier relentless pacing was a still life compared to his reaction now. He exploded, arms windmilling as quickly as his mind whirled. Plan? What plan had he come up with? He couldn't remember a thing.

"What are you talking about, you demented man?" Weasel demanded, before another thought occurred. "And who's Esme?"

Rasten frowned at him. "Esme was the queen of your drunkenness last night, little man. The barman's daughter."

Weasel stopped for a moment. "Wait a minute… she wasn't a serving wench? No wonder old Tubman was so harsh with the cold water this morning if that was his daughter…"

"Hmm," murmured Rasten. "You treated her abominably."

Weasel caught himself nodding, before cocking an eyebrow and firing a quick glance at his companion. "True," he concurred, "but then I always do."

Rasten resolutely refused to smile. Sometimes he found life with this razor-witted young man a genuine pleasure, for where Weasel went, laughter often followed. Other times, however, Rasten found himself silently offering up a prayer, asking Tal Rasha to forgive his wayward friend.

He knew such prayers were wasted on Weasel, for the southerner held as much belief in the gods as he did in the idea of an honest day's labor – such things were for other people.

"Anyway," said Weasel. "I still don't remember any plan. I'm sure I would have remembered a plan. I always remember those."

"Except this time," countered Rasten. "I didn't quite catch all of it myself. It was hard to hear when you were talking into Esme's chest."

Weasel shrugged. "Well, you have to admit, it was a very nice chest. But did I catch that right, this plan you are staking our lives on… no, more important than that… my life on is one which you didn't quite hear?"

"I got the gist of it, and Esme told me the rest while you were sloughing off your hangover."

"Go on," said Weasel, continuing his pacing, one ear cocked towards Rasten, the other towards the squeak from his boots that wouldn't quite go away.

"You told her it would be just like that time you were caught in the bedchamber of the mayor's wife in Carolay. There you were…"

"That wasn't me, it was Ulrith Griffinfriend as you well know."

"Not last night it wasn't, it was all the work of the humble Weasel, serf's son turned guest of kings. You want to take the credit, then it's only your own fault when people believe you."

Weasel curled his lip. "They were peasants. Of course they believe me. I've conned the best in the land before now, I'm sure a serving wench and a room full of drunkards is still within my compass."

Rasten had finished unwrapping the package, and now set down its contents carefully, half a dozen javelins, which he placed in easy reach against the wall.

He continued: "So, there you – or Ulrith – were, when the mayor and his cadre of bodyguards opened the door to find you in the throes of ecstasy with his beloved… what was her name?"

"Mimi," supplied Weasel helpfully. "And if Ulrith is to be believed, then next time we reach Carolay, I really really must introduce myself."

"Yes, so when you were caught, and despite having only the remnants of some leather trews around your ankles as armor, you managed to fend off the attentions of the outraged mayor, his excessively keen troop of bodyguards and the as yet unsatisfied Mimi until all of them had been driven back out of the door. Mimi included."

Weasel stopped and scratched at his head.

"OK, Rasten, let me get this clear. We're basing our defense of this gods-forsaken village upon a story I drunkenly told a serving girl who I was trying to get into bed, a story which itself was told to us by Ulrith, a barbarian who hasn't had a sober day as long as I've known him."

Rasten nodded. "I can see it's coming back to you. But let me fill you in on the rest, for you were long lost to sleep when Esme and I worked out the details…"

Weasel listened, and though he still hated the odds, he had to admit that as plans went, he'd come up with a good one.

* * *

The six-limbed Reavers skittered into the canyon cautiously, their pale, doughy skin blistering in the heat of the day. As warbands went, it wasn't the biggest that Dhoka had commanded, but it was more than ample for the task at hand. The village hadn't long brought in its harvest, and the Reavers needed food to take back to the sunless lands below the desert.

Dhoka raised her forehand and waved the others forward. The sooner this task was done, the sooner they would be out of this accursed heat and light and restored once more to the cool serenity of the warren.

They edged down Hook Canyon, the walls thankfully offering up the shade her men craved. Without urging, the warband moved close to the towering sides. Dhoka followed on, grateful for the shadow herself. Traveling in the full light of the day would have taken too much out of the warriors, and left them dizzied and disoriented ahead of the anticipated battle that early evening would bring.

While the opposition wasn't going to be worth mentioning, Dhoka still didn't want to take any risks with the condition of her troops. That was the way mistakes happened.

Before long, the warband neared the tight, narrow bend that gave the canyon its name, and it was only when the first javelins struck her forward scouts that Dhoka became aware of the two armored warriors stood right in the teeth of Hook Canyon.

* * *

"Ha! Two down," cried Weasel as the first javelins struck home on the insectoid Reavers, and he snatched up the next one greedily.

"Two down," Rasten concurred, "only another score to go."

Weasel sighed. "Rasten, we're still about to die. Can't you just enjoy the little successes?"

"Agreed," grunted the taller man, as he let fly with the second javelin.

Used correctly, surprise is a potent weapon. By the time the Reavers had realized what was happening, the two had loosed their supply of javelins into the warband, and fled around the curve of Hook Canyon, where the rocky walls narrowed to little wider than the double doors to the bedchamber of far-distant Mimi. This was the second part of the plan, to reduce the odds by stopping too many combatants from attacking at once, and Weasel and Rasten scampered into place.

Dhoka cursed, and numbered her dead. Four slain by the short spears, one not far off and another with the joint for his weapon arms pierced. Useless. Dhoka snapped an order, and while half her troops readied their bows, the others fell upon the dead and wounded, finishing the task and scooping out the brains of the fallen. Dhoka's lieutenant, Tjoda, brought them to her when the troops had finished.

Those who had fallen had been much closer to the enemy than Dhoka. As she ingested the organs, and tasted their memories, she pondered the next move.

* * *

"Four down, I make it," gasped Weasel, resting against the wall.

"Six," said Rasten. "The Reavers finish their fallen. The two we wounded will play no further part in this matter."

"Not a very sensible way of doing things," said Weasel, drawing his two short swords. Setting them both down, he next drew from a pouch on his belt a small vial filled with a black, unctuous fluid which he carefully applied to each blade, a faint, musky smell of old fish accompanying its presence.

Rasten eyed the poison with some disdain, reaching back and drawing his mighty two-handed sword from his back. Weasel caught the look and again cocked an eyebrow at his more muscular companion.

"Look," he said. "If I could pick one of those things up, then I might find a use for it, but you've got the brawn to drive that through the toughest hide. Me, I've got to improvise. And if improvising keeps you alive, and better yet me, then we'll both be thankful."

There were other things Weasel left unsaid about the oozing liquid, things he knew Rasten wouldn't approve of, about how the liquid was one of the most potent on the market, said to kill men by driving them mad with terror, and in no short order. Used skilfully, an assassin could use drops of it to mimic a heart attack. Here, however, there would be no need for subtlety. Weasel glanced back at Rasten. "Any other habits the Reavers have I should know about?"

"Yes," said Rasten. "they'll send in a lone scout next. The Reavers consume the memories of their fallen, so even if we hurt the scout badly, we can't let it get away. I'll fall back to lure it in, while you take up your hiding place. When you make your strike, I'll join you."

Rasten was right. Dhoka sent in a scout as her next move. Rasten made a show of running away down the canyon, and, properly baited, that was enough for the Reaver to slip around the hook.

By every code of honor, Weasel should have announced his presence before stepping out behind the Reaver and executing a double sweep of his blades. Weasel, however, put honor and duty in the same box as the gods, so the first thing the Reaver warrior knew was when Weasel's blades bit deep into the scout's spine and pain spasmed up his body.

Weasel stepped back, satisfied. It was only when he looked up to see Rasten charging back up the canyon, yelling for him to look out that a note of concern began to edge across Weasel's face. But by then, it was too late. For he could only watch as the Reaver dropped down onto its front four limbs and launched its rear legs backwards, straight into Weasel's stomach, sending him flying into the canyon wall. Somehow, he held onto his swords, and raised them instinctively to fend off the expected attack, but he could only watch as the Reaver, trailing blood and the remnants of what Weasel had presumed was its backbone, turned and skittered at high speed out of the canyon.

"I told you we couldn't let it get away," said Rasten, when he caught up. "So why did you let it escape?"

Weasel coughed, and sat up.

"First of all, Rasten, might I point out that you didn't warn me they could do that. Second of all, might I also add that I'm feeling a certain lack of sympathy here. That thing had a kick on it that the mule you insist on riding everywhere would be proud of. Lastly," he said, hefting one of his swords. "that thing's not going very far at all."

* * *

Dhoka saw the scout return, but it only made it halfway to the rest of the warband before it collapsed, writhing in pain. Again, Dhoka barked a command and two of the warriors retrieved the scout from here it lay. By the time, they brought him to Dhoka, the scout had died.

"Give me his thoughts," she snapped. Dhoka needed to know what the scout had seen. As she raised the scout's brain to her lips, she anticipated the ending of this battle in short order. Tasting his memories, she almost laughed as she saw the opposition really did only number two, and one of those foolish enough to get caught by the snap of a hindlimb. She smiled, and prepared to order her warriors to attack as one, to overwhelm these whelps who presumed they could stop a Reaver warband.

But then she stopped, the words frozen in her craw, as she sipped on a bad memory. All she could see in her mind was the blackencrusted blades wielded by the little man. Her senses caught a faint, musky smell of old fish... as she reached the memory of the terror that the scout felt thanks to that liquid. And then she screamed.

* * *

Not even Rasten had ever heard a Reaver scream. Before either of them knew it, both Rasten and Weasel were peering back around the hook, looking with some confusion as Dhoka collapsed to the floor, her forelimbs clutching at her throat. As they watched, her flailing movements became less fevered, until they subsided completely, and the warband gathered around their fallen leader, confused and, suddenly, fearful.

Tjoda, however, stepped forward. He knew what must be done, for he had seen Dhoka do as much many times. He was the first of the remaining warband to reach down and start to taste her memories.

* * *

When sunset fell on the little village of Mora's Calm, all the villagers' eyes turned eastward to the end of Hook Canyon. Hands tightened around improvised weapons, and all waited for the end.

After all, heroes or not, no two men could stop an entire Reaver warband.

And then, from out of the last rays of sunshine, the villagers could see two men striding out of the canyon.

Weasel and Rasten walked, laughing, into the village and past the demanding voices of the locals until they were settled in front of the bar, with Tubman pouring out the ale.

Having put off the questions as long as possible – along with the comments about how neither of them had a scratch on them, although a few commented that Weasel's armor looked… dented,

Weasel finally coughed and stood up.

He raised his tankard, slipped an arm around the willing shoulders of Esme, and cried out: "A toast! A toast! Here's to Reavers. They may be fine warriors, but thank the gods their eye will always be bigger than the things they can stomach!"

Tales From The Mists Foreword

"The oldest and strongest emotion of mankind is fear, and the oldest and strongest kind of fear is the fear of the unknown."
– H. P. Lovecraft.

We fear that which we do not know. We fear the monsters that lurk in the mists. What can we know of the creatures which dwell under the crusts of the earth — what of the serpents that slumber beneath the seas? We fear the terror that hides amongst twisted trees and black jungles and we fear what lurks beyond the veil of death.

Our first story, by Leo McBride, takes us into those twisted trees in search of The Chickcharney, a creature of Bahamian legend, as a young girl is brought face-to-face with the truth behind the myth.

Ricardo Victoria gives us a glimpse into drug-addled madness in Bone Peyote, a compelling narrative which takes place during the Mexican celebration of Dia de Muertos, the Day of the Dead. The Old Ones mix with old traditions as the two converge to a chilling conclusion: the Old Ones are still with us, devouring us, a permanent fixture within the cityscape itself, and you are its next meal.

Morgan Porter, fresh meat in this group of story-tellers, offers a classic Lovecraftian narration from the depths below. There is more to what this story suggests, so be on the lookout for hidden clues to unearth this story's underlying message about the horrors that lie beneath the surface. The true monsters in this tale may surprise you.

If you have ever hated your boss at your job, then our very own Mary Shelley — Alei Kotdaishura, offers us a real monster none of us can escape. Work is horror and this boss is to die for — unless you are the heroine in Beast, who may just relish her new work assignment a little too much.

Finally, before your passage to the other side ends, our last story by author Brent A. Harris brings a homage to science fiction gone wrong and a nod to The Twilight Zone. He offers a psychological thriller in a world where Death may no longer touch us. But in this world, there may be a fate far worse than death — a fate our intrepid computer programmer, Richard

Rigby, realizes all too late that he cannot escape. Or is it all just in his head?

Join us in our journey into the deepest cracks of the mind, as we delve into these stories of the strange and the cerebral. Read our words, dive into the abyss of blackness. But before you do, heed our caution: You are about to turn a page into the unknown.

The Chickcharney
By Leo McBride

I saw the dust rising before I saw the men coming. It was a good ten minutes after the reddish haze rose that the truck rattled to a stop in the yard outside the half-built fishing lodge, its engine ticking as it tried to cool off under the hot Bahamian sun.

Samora frowned in the truck's direction as the door clunked open.

"Een nothin' good here," he muttered, his voice low enough not to carry far. But I heard. "Child, don't let your mout carry you, y'hear?" he hissed. I nodded and picked at the edge of my dress.

The man stepped out of the truck. Samora didn't move from where he sat on the partially-constructed veranda that would circle the lodge when it was finished. I nestled on the bottom step below.

He waited as the man wafted his hat to clear some of the dust still drifting around the parked vehicle, then signaled to the three men riding in its flatbed to get out.

He tapped his sunglasses with his finger as he walked towards us.

"Where's the foreman?" he asked to the air, not looking at Samora and most certainly not looking at me.

Samora waited, shrugged before replying: "I een know who you mean, general. You want who's in charge?"

The man looked back at Samora sharply at that, his tap-taptapping finger stopping, before he removed his sunglasses. "No," he said sternly. "I'm Osterman. And I'm the man in charge."

I looked up at Samora, who looked briefly back, that warning look in his eyes, and sighed. This was going to be trouble.

They argued for a while. I didn't think Mr Osterman even noticed me, he was so busy shouting at Samora. I began to wish that maybe I should have done as Mama had said that morning and not crept away to the site. I'd watched it every day since they began cutting down the pines - each morning before Mama stirred for school if I could, each afternoon when coming home in the time before Mama returned. They started so quick, I thought they'd be done in a week.

Samora was our neighbor and the only one on the crew I knew. The rest all came in to Andros from other islands, some from other countries. He seemed so happy when the work started, he'd been idle for a while, but the week became two and the lightness in his smile dimmed. The two became three, a month, more.

"Child, they don't know what they're doing," he said to me on the porch one evening. "They use strangers' ways."

He wasn't trying to argue, but this Mr Osterman wasn't finding peace in what Samora had to say. Why wasn't the work closer to being finished, the man demanded. Where was Hannity, who was supposed to be on the site, he growled. Why was the toolbox sat at the bottom of the steps half empty? Why was the digger sitting idle with its engine cover open? Why... why... why?

Samora tried and tried to answer the questions, but no answer was ever enough. The man kept driving and driving at him. The more I saw, the more my mouth strained to open, to speak up for him.

"Don't let your mout carry you..." his words lingered in my head, his warning to stay quiet, but I hated seeing him like this. Suddenly, the man strode up the steps, making me scurry out of the way. He barged past Samora on the platform and grabbed part of the framework of the building, stabbing his other finger at a broken strut.

"Look," he was shouting, "even the work you have done is shoddy, it's falling apart. Who did this? Who did it? Was it you? Was it? Well?"

Samora was shaking his head, his hands half raised in a placating measure, trying to find an answer that would suit this man who had barged into our afternoon. And then there was an answer that made them both stop, an answer that surprised me as much as it did them, for it came from my mouth.

"The chicks did it!" I cried aloud, and I think that was the first time Mr Osterman had looked at me.

Mr Osterman took two steps down the stairs to the veranda. I lowered my eyes but he quickly snapped: "Look at me, girl."

I kept my eyes low, but he spoke again, more sternly. Samora started to speak but Mr Osterman cut him off with a wave of his hand. "What's her name?" he quickly asked Samora, as if I wasn't even there to answer for myself.

"Cara," Samora replied.

"Well, Cara," said Mr Osterman, "seeing as you think you can interrupt me, what the hell are you talking about?"

I looked up, afraid. I stole a look over at Samora, whose warning eyes tried to tell me to stop, to be silent, to not tell. But I couldn't help it, and the words spilled out.

I told Mr Osterman everything. I told him all that Samora had told me each evening on the porch outside Mama's house. How things had started to go wrong from the moment they started chopping down the pine trees at the site. First, it was tools being misplaced.

Samora had told me how they would put a tool down for a moment, only to turn and find them gone. Then it was problems with the generator. One morning, Samora said, they found the wires of the Jeep shredded. A wild animal, the foreman Hannity had insisted. A troublemaker, the off-island workers had muttered. Then the first of those workers failed to show up for the job one morning, and I remember that night as Samora nursed his rum on the porch and the look in his eyes as Mama said to him: "We both know it een no animal."

He had nodded and said a word for the first time when talking about the troubles at the site.

"Chickcharney."

"Chickcharney?" asked Mr Osterman, his accent sounding out the word differently from the way Mama said it, from the way I said it, from the way Samora had said it on the porch that night. "What the hell is a Chickcharney?"

When I was younger, growing up at Mama's knee, she used to tell me the stories. The Chickcharney was the creature of the forest. Mama taught me to treat the Chickcharney well if you wanted it to treat you the same. Not everyone learned that lesson. Get up to mischief, she would say, and the Chickcharney will get up to mischief with you.

She told me of her own grandmother, who worked as a maid at a British man's estate. He would march up and down giving orders, she said, trying to set up a sisal plantation, not caring for the words of those who knew the land, not listening to the words of caution whispered to him that he would bring the bad luck of the Chickcharney upon himself, that such a curse can never be shaken off.

The young man, an arrogant soul named Chamberlain, tried and failed for six years to create that plantation, before slinking back to London and the life of a politician, and one at that whose name was never spoken of with pride. Mama would tell me these stories over dinner and then, together, we would put a share of the meal on an old dish and leave it outside, balanced on a rock by the edge of the trees.

Sometimes I would even leave out a little trinket or two, a toy, a plaything. The Chickcharney's share, she would say.

"See a chick and it will bring good luck for all your days. Lor' knows we could use such luck."

We would stand together and peer towards the woods until the light faded but not once did we see the chicks. But every morning when we came out again, whatever we had left was gone.

I didn't tell Mr Osterman this. How do you begin to tell someone who thinks they know so much that they know so little? I was saved by Samora.

"It's just a folk tale," he said. "Beasts who look like owls and live in the trees of Andros, making trouble where they can."

Mr Osterman frowned his way. "I don't have time for this," he snarled. "Now, where is Hannity?"

Samora had spared me for now. "He left," replied Samora. "Two days ago to go fetch the lumber from the dock. We thought maybe he bust up a wheel on a pothole in the road and that's why he didn't get back yesterday. But there's been no sign today. He took the last of the other workers with him, tol' me to keep a watch on tings here."

"You know the way to this dock?" demanded Mr Osterman.

"Kinda, I could drive you there in the morning," said Samora.

"Nonsense," came the reply. "You'll drive me there now."

At 13 years old, I was old enough to walk home myself from the site. I'd tried to tell Samora, but he insisted that Mama would never forgive him if he let me. So I found myself on the bench seat inside the truck as it bounded along the battered track that led towards the dock, Mr Osterman at the wheel and Samora to one side. I could see him sulking, wishing he wasn't there. For me, it was an adventure. I hunched forward, peering ahead. The dock was a place of work, not for a young girl, so the road ahead, old and battered, was new to me.

In the back rode one of the other men that had arrived in the truck, a silent man from Long Cay whose name, Thomas, we only knew because that was what Mr Osterman had bellowed at him when he told him to climb in the back. The other two remained behind.

The light was fading when we saw it. The truck that Hannity and the three other men had driven two days ago, was just off the side of the road, jerked to one side at a strange angle and with its load of timber scattered on the ground around it.

Mr Osterman swore, making me duck my head by reflex for the kind of swish of the hand that Mama would have given me at home if I'd said that word. Then he pulled the car to the side of the track, and switched on the headlights.

We could easily see the burst tire of the truck with the headlights on. One of the doors stood open too.

"Thomas!" bellowed Mr Osterman as he climbed out of the truck, grabbing a flashlight from the well of the seat as he did. Thomas clambered down from the flatbed and joined his employer as he headed over to the other vehicle.

Samora fixed me with one of his stern looks, the kind he tried to put on when he thought he could order me around. "Don' een mess with me, child," he said. "You stay right here." And with that, he climbed out of the truck.

I counted to ten. And then followed.

There was more than a burst tyre stopping Hannity's truck from getting back on the road. The weight of the lumber and the crunch off the road left the rear looking buckled. Thomas had scooted as far as he dared under the back of the vehicle before sliding back out and shaking his head to Mr Osterman. Samora hung back, shining a flashlight wherever it was useful and scowling at me for disobeying his instructions.

"Well, if this is their truck, where are they?" demanded Mr Osterman, looking through the front seats and finding nothing but the odd wrapper of a candy bar and crumpled receipts from the store out by the dock.

Samora shrugged, flicking his light around the area with little enthusiasm. But the light caught on something and without thinking, I pointed. Mr Osterman followed my gaze and pointed his own flashlight in the same direction. Footprints, clear to see in the dusty earth, headed towards the nearby trees.

I looked up towards the pine woods, a dark mass reaching for the sky in this early evening half-light and for the first time felt a shiver.

The trees were knotted thick and close, some even tangled together at their tops. I could almost feel the woods as a presence, watching, waiting. "If this happened earlier today," said Mr Osterman, "maybe they went into the trees for some shade from this damned hot sun you have here."

Samora stirred uneasily. "Maybe we'd be best coming back..." he started.

"Nonsense," interrupted Mr Osterman. "We're here now, we might as well have a look."

And with that, he first turned off his truck's lights, then led the way towards the woods, Thomas at his heels. Samora grabbed my hand and, reluctantly, started to follow.

Inside the tree line, my shiver became a chill. I edged closer to Samora, worried now by the darkness. There was a trail of sorts and the footprints of the four men could still be seen enough to track their path. Thomas proved especially apt at spotting the treads, and soon was leading the way, Mr Osterman just behind him and Samora and I bringing up the rear.

We had been walking for perhaps 15 minutes when Samora finally spoke up. "This is far enough," he said. "We can't keep going into the forest, we'll never find our way back out."

Mr Osterman stopped and looked back at us, where I sheltered slightly behind Samora's leg.

"We followed the footprints in," said Mr Osterman. "We can follow the footprints out. It'll be easier, our trail will be there too."

Samora shuffled slightly in his place before speaking up again. "It's getting darker, we might not be able to find the trail."

"Nonsense," scowled Mr Osterman. "Look, come with me."

He walked back about 30 yards, beckoning us to follow him. We did, and he pointed out the trail of footprints. Then, suddenly, he came to a halt. "This is odd," he said.

I looked up at Samora, who gripped my hand a little more tightly, then led us forward. We looked down at the ground, where our footprints had only just been, where the trail we had followed had led us this way. It looked different, somehow. I peered closer, edging slightly away from Samora to see better. It looked... brushed. Swept.

As if Mama had come by with her broom and wiped away all trace of someone passing by.

I shrank back, tightening my grip on Samora again, squeezing so hard I thought maybe I might hurt him but when I looked up, his face was a blank mask. I'd seen him like this before, on the porch, in those times between jobs, when times were tough. He always put on a show at times like that but deep down, I knew, he was on edge. Scared.

Mr Osterman spoke up again. "I can't find any sign of the footprints any more. What the devil? Thomas! Come and see if you can find the trail. Thomas? Get over here."

We turned around. Thomas was gone.

"We have to leave," said Samora. "Now."

Mr Osterman shrugged. "Leave? Come on, don't be ridiculous. Thomas has to be around here somewhere."

He raised his voice and shouted the missing man's name but the woods seemed to deaden the sound, the echo dying away fast in the close-pressed pine trees. Mr Osterman called again. And again. But only silence came back. I wouldn't even know what Thomas' voice sounded like, I thought, I never even heard him speak.

"Mr Osterman, we have to..." began Samora but was cut off by the snap of the other man's voice.

"You'll leave when I damn well say you leave. I told you I was in charge, that is my lodge and you get paid by me. You leave now and you can forget getting your money."

Samora started to answer, but bit his tongue. I could feel him bubbling away next to me, wanting to burst out and say what he thought but not daring to. I didn't have any such reason to hold back.

"This is all your fault," I shouted. "Yours. You're the one intruding. You're the one who didn't try to understand that it wasn't your land!"

Mr Osterman snarled back. "It damn well is my land. I bought it, I paid for it, I have plans for it!"

"No!" I screamed, my voice shrill in the night air. "You don't own the land just because you bought it. You don't belong just because you have papers that say so. The land was there before you, and so were the chicks. You didn't respect them, and now we're trapped here because of you. It's all your fault!"

With that, I turned and ran, slipping my hand from Samora and dashing blindly away. I didn't know where I was but suddenly I didn't care, I just had to be far from that man. I heard someone crashing through the woods behind me and glanced back to see Mr Osterman chasing me, a snarl upon his face. Samora started after him to stop him but stumbled and fell. Mr Osterman plunged on in my wake. I could hear him shouting angry words, I could hear him threatening me, I could hear him swearing and crashing his way through the trees behind me.

The woods seemed to rear up in front of me and finding a path through the trees became harder. Finally, I came to a stop, gasping hard for air. I turned and there he loomed, marching towards me and raising his hand holding his flashlight up in the air as if getting ready to strike me.

The light swung wildly up, and in that moment, I saw it. The birdlike figure swooped down from the tree above his head, three-fingered arms reaching out and locking around his face. I tried to gasp out a warning, but Mr Osterman's arm swung down, and I felt a sharp pain as the flashlight cracked against my head.

Everything seemed to swirl in my vision, but I saw as those arms gave a sharp twist, I heard the sudden snap and Mr Osterman crumpled to the ground.

I screamed at the sight, and the creature's head swiveled around, revealing its piercing red eyes. It folded itself down from the tree, its long pale legs thudding onto the earth, and turned towards me. Again, I screamed, and as it walked towards me, I suddenly felt the darkness growing around me, the world spinning and then, a moment more, and it all went black.

That's how Samora found me, he told me. He had followed the sounds through the forest and found me lying in the middle of a clearing turned on my side. He said it was the same way someone would lie you down if they were trying to help you recover. I don't know what he really meant by that. He had carried me back to the road. He said he had just followed wherever the clearest gaps were in the trees and we had emerged not far from the truck.

We got in the truck and drove back to Mama's, which is where I woke, with Samora and Mama crowded round me in concern. The next morning, he went back to the scene with some others from the island and they searched for Mr Osterman and the others, but no one could find any trace of them.

It was as if the island had swallowed them up, he told me later. I didn't tell him until that night about what I had seen, and then I confessed it all as we sat on the porch, the owl-like creature with the curved, three-fingered hands, the glowing red eyes. I thought he would laugh at me, tell me I was wrong, but he just nodded, put his hand over my shaking fists and said to be calm.

"They say if you see a Chickcharney you'll be blessed with good fortune," he said. "I know of no way other than luck that we got out of those woods. When we were out there, and I was too afraid to say anything, you did what I couldn't, you stood up for the two of us."

He paused, and looked away from the porch towards the woods.

"You protected us. And something protected you. Osterman threatened us. And something stopped him. I een know how to say it any different but the way your Mama says it. Treat the Chickcharney well, and it will treat you well. But cross it and it'll get up to mischief with you. Seems to me you were on the right side of whatever you saw."

We sat there for a while until the sky got darker and we moved inside, away from the uncomfortable remembrance of our race through the woods. But we both came back outside briefly. Samora and Mama both walked with me as I carried a plate of food to the edge of the woods, where I balanced it on a rock. "Thank you," I whispered to the trees before we returned to our houses and waited to see what the morning would bring.

Bone Peyote

By Ricardo Victoria

If I knew then what I know now, I would look at the traditions of my native land with a different perspective, one more of awe than morbid curiosity. Everything happened six months ago, during the autumn, when I came back from my studies abroad for some rest. I took the opportunity then, to bask in what I considered one of the most unique celebrations of my native Mexico: The Day of the Dead, held on the first and second of November, just after Halloween.

It is a date full of vibrant colours, music and flavours. Contrary to the name, it is a celebration of both the living and the dead.

Mexicans, probably due to history or to some atavistic condition, tend to have a dark sense of humour that is best expressed when we laugh at Death. The Catrina, a stiff upper-lipped and well-dressed female Grim Reaper becomes the main character in a day where, tradition dictates, the dead come back from the grave in spirit, to visit their relatives and eat the offerings left behind for them.

Families, be it in cemeteries, caves or inside their homes, build homemade altars, where photographs, candies, fruit liqueur, food, Grim Reaper representations in funny situations, magazines and toys are left for two days so the beloved departed could enjoy the love of the living.

The tradition backs from pre-Columbian days, although nowadays it is a syncretic event that mixes ancient traditions with the deep-seated Catholic beliefs of the general population. And in recent years, it fights the invasion of Halloween by adding some of its tenets into this schizophrenic mix.

But I digress, the Day of the Dead shares, at least in the most mystical sense, the same concept of the Samhain: the idea that the veil that separates the realms of the dead from the living, the spiritual from the material and the otherworldly dimensions from the mundane is thin enough to be crossed. Usually, it is the dead that make the journey rather than the living. But that hasn't stopped some of the more reckless or adventurous living people from trying to make a similar journey in the other direction and live to tell the tale.

And in a country deeply embedded in mystical traditions, stories of human sacrifices and warlocks that can shape shift into animals to steal your spirit; and a country regarded as one of the most haunted due to its bloody and convoluted history, populated with some of the weirdest deities of ancient pantheons - there is no lack of method nor legends about how to do it.

As I said before, I was returning home from abroad, where I was studying something that, in light of the revelations learned, pales in comparison. I traded the crispy leaves and the rainy days mixed with the bonfires of the Midlands in England, for the smell of copal (which is similar to incense and fulfils a similar function in local traditions) and the full spectrum of colours of the alfeñique (toys made of sugarcane) of the massive, overpopulated Mexico City, a behemoth of a place, whose innards full of tunnels for the subway cross the remains of the lake upon which the city was built in times of the Aztec.

I was planning to meet with a friend, Julian, in his flat, before going back to my hometown, forty-five minutes by motorway from Mexico City, planning to hear his stories from his recent trip into the so-called mystical land of Real de Catorce, an old colonial town in the north-central region of the country, known for rather lousy Hollywoodesque movies and the promise of mystical, magical tours to meet with shamans, the local wise men, and to eat peyote, a small, spineless cactus with psychoactive alkaloids, particularly mescaline that, according to their traditions, allowed one to take a trip into the other realms. This was popularized by a series of books, one entitled 'Of other realities and dreams', by an author whose name I can't recall right now. In that book, he narrated how a very strange and quirky shaman taught him how to commute with the spirits of the land through the use of the peyote.

Over the past decades and since the publication of said book, peyote had been all the rage, be it by fashion or be it due to more spiritual endeavours, to achieve that kind of experience. Now, the reader might think that I dismiss such activities as foolish, thanks to the tone in of this text. But on the contrary, those that know me know that I have a keen interest, some would say morbid even, with stories of the strange and the occult, with the Day of Dead and other realities.

At first dismissed as a childish interest, it informed several of my personal tastes, mainly due to the old stories on of an ancestor who fought in the Mexican War for Independence with the rebels and witnessed weird events while hiding for a season or two in the caves of the Veracruz mountain range, a place known for its warlocks and witches who cast both fortunes and curses if the payments are good enough… and sometimes, such payment wasn't necessarily made with money, as humans have other valuable things to use as payment.

My ancestor recorded the events in a diary that is hidden amongst many books in my grandfather's personal library and I have to admit that I read it several times, hidden during the night until I memorized it. It was this obsession with those stories that led me to the path to meet and befriend Julian. A kid from a family of considerable financial resources but poor emotional contact, Julian solved the issue of his birth handicap, a lame leg, with his quest for paths to enlightenment… or so he said. At times, I thought it was more an excuse to get high, bed a girl or engage in new ways of debauchery.

Our friendship was born from a shared interest in weird stories and urban legends of the country as well as the story of my ancestor (Julian kept swearing that it was his ancestor as well and as such we were distant relatives, a claim that I used to doubt until now) and it was kept alive despite the distance.

Recently, Julian decided to celebrate his birthday, which coincided with the start of the autumn season, with a trip to Real de Catorce. He said that he was looking for the shaman mentioned in that book whose author's name still eludes me. In his emails, probably sent from a local cyber coffee shop, he sounded excited, as his search apparently bore fruit. Not in the way he expected, but apparently in one that promised more interesting venues for his 'quest'. It seemed that while he didn't find the original shaman from the book, he found an old man who claimed to be his student, but who later diverged into more obscure and powerful rites that made what was described in the book look like child's play.

Of course, those rites attracted the scorn of the locals, as apparently some of the cats and goats of a couple of ranchers disappeared and more concerning rumours talked about a Canadian couple that no one saw again after they went for a walkabout with the old man on a cold day in December; and as a consequence of the unsavoury rumours, the old man lived in a meagre, dilapidated hut outside the town, alone. The authorities tried to confirm the rumours, especially because of the couple's disappearance, but between the well-paid corruption and the lack of proper evidence, such investigation never came to fruition. None of this, however, deterred Julian. On the contrary, it seemed to spur him on even more. My belief back then was that he was trying to prove something to the world, as the lameness in his leg became worse and his parents left him to his own devices.

The empty vastness surrounding that mine town proved an excellent place for Julian to test such rites. And with each test, his emails became more and more excited… at first. Once he moved from the delight of finding a proper teacher to the initial lessons on those rites, he started to write on his most meaningful experiences and their results.

"Most people believe, my dear friend…" he wrote "that this world is but a single reality of linear time, where we are the centre of the universe. How wrong they are. Our reality is just one of many; deepseated layers overlapping, interconnected in strings of Mobius-like architecture. Your admired teacher has only hinted at this with his crude equations in that book on manifolds and n-dimensions, but his understanding is still crude and primitive. The truth can only be revealed if one is willing to expand their minds with those peyote plants. My mentor is teaching me ways that the other book barely mentioned."

When I asked him about the rumours surrounding his mentor, Julian dismissed them with claims about how ignorant the other people were. The next emails contained similar replies, of more metaphysical character, explaining to me that time and space were not only the same, but were easily traversed in any direction, past and future, just as it was to cross the veil that served as seal between the mundane world and the otherworld that he started to call Mictlán, as in the land of the dead of the Aztec religion.

"My mentor has provided me with a new ritual and a very scarce type of peyote, called 'bone peyote', which locals said originally grew from the bones of a dead deity. And how much I have learned from it!"

Another mail read, "Those stories that we dismissed as mere mythology in school… hold more truths than modern science is willing to admit. Oh how wonderful it would be if the scholars admired those stone calendars in the museums with new eyes! The world is not built on cyclic periods, but it's more like a spiral whose end is the beginning. Those calendars have to be seen under the influence of this variety, as would allow you to unlock the fourth and fifth and sixth dimension carved in those stones. No wonder why the Mayans in Yucatán invented the zero, if they were familiar with the true nature of reality."

After that email, Julian said that he wanted to try a new rite, one that would allow him to travel properly, more than just observe, through space and time. But his mentor had disappeared a day before with his whereabouts unknown.

Julian suspected that he went on a walkabout in the desert and a freak sandstorm must have caught him.

Julian waited for a couple of days, but there were no signs of his return. The locals took their own action and asked the authorities to declare him dead, burning the hut at once. With nowhere to stay, Julian decided to carry out the rite on the date that sounded most promising: the Day of the Dead, just when, according to tradition, the veil that separates the land of the dead and the living is thin enough to allow the crossing.

Thus I waited for Julian on a cold morning on the First of November, Day of all Saints, the major day of the festival outside the infamous market of Sonora. Hidden beneath its traditional market visage, in that place was located one of the main hubs in Mexico City for those that practice the occult arts or wished to acquire the supplies needed for mysterious rituals. Julian arrived with his usual gait and a new cane with a metal handle, which I assumed was made of silver. Julian was particularly happy, yapping and mumbling about this new rite and how he needed me there to record his visions in his diary, as his voice recorder stopped working properly after his last experience.

He took me along the narrow aisles of the market until we reached the shops that sold the paraphernalia to fend off bad mojo, create love potions, curse your enemies and create rituals of prosperity or decay. Julian kept asking several of the vendors for some very specific items and the bone peyote he needed, though only one agreed to sell the items, as most of them said that he was mad. And the one that agreed to sell only did it after crossing himself at least seven times after receiving a hefty sum of money.

"Fools!" Julian said. "Their saints and silly superstitions kept them away from the truth. Their parlour tricks are nothing compared to what I've seen. The priests from the Aztec, the Toltec and the Mayan, all of them knew the truth and that scared the Spaniards and shook their beliefs."

That last part concerned me. While Julian wasn't exactly a practicing Catholic, he never dismissed it in such a way. It was as if his recent experiences had emboldened him to the point of cockiness and reckless hubris. I tried to ignore the warnings in my head, but they nagged me all day. If only I had listened.

We spent the rest of the day eating, buying candy skulls and trading stories of our respective lives up to that point. In comparison, my studies seemed childish against the secrets that Julian uncovered.

The expansive alternate dimensions that are placed beyond the veil that split the living from the dead were vast and rich, making ours just but a humble reflection, tied by our preconceptions of time and space. In those places, time was meaningless, allowing you to see past, present and future at once and travel freely amongst them.

Julian insisted that the old traditions hidden behind the coat of commercial celebrations such as the Day of Dead were true and that the spirits did come to visit us in this night when the crossing was possible.

It was only at this time of the year that it was possible for humans to travel the other way - using the right tools, as shown by many legends and folklore from around the world. He claimed that the rite he was going to use tonight would allow him to travel, at least in a spiritual sense, rather than just having visions. He said that for those realms the flesh was anathema, the safest way to travel was in spiritual form, or risk entering and being torn asunder by the flows of contradicting time. That reminded me of those folk tales where someone is dragged by a spirit to their otherworldly realms and, when they tried to return, our linear time caught up with them, turning them into dust in a matter of days or hours.

Thus I found it reasonable that Julian accounted for that even if by now I was starting to dismiss his speech as the product of heavy psychotropic drug overuse. I was surprised, going by his description of the rites he had practiced, at the amounts of the special peyote he had consumed in short time and started to fear it may have affected his brain. I tried to turn the conversation during our visit to Mexico City and how the syncretic clash of modernity and ancient customs took place in each corner of the historic downtown, about the renovation of the Templo Mayor, the ancient Aztec temple situated right in the middle of the city. Or the plans for the new airport and how the digging of the foundations had encountered some technical difficulties. I tried to talk him into more friendly topics but it was to no avail.

It was only when I asked him about the circumstances of the disappearance of his new mentor that I saw a silent coolness overcome him. He claimed that what happened had a simpler explanation, instead of suspicions he shared in his emails. He even dismissed with disdain what the locals reported to the newspaper as foolish tales of ignorant people.

"He wasn't taken by the spirits during a rite… oh no." He said, with a very unconvincing tone. "He was an old man who took needless risks going on walkabouts at the wee hours of the day. He probably broke a leg, after all he was a really old man. The sandstorm was just a coincidence that stopped him from getting rescued. He died there in the desert." Julian proclaimed with certainty in his voice. But when I pressed, asking him why he didn't take it upon himself to search for his mentor, his voice trembled about how his lame leg didn't allow for that and he still had great things to do. I smelled bullshit as he was always one to take physical risks despite his leg. It was then when he finally acceded to change topics and asked me about my work.

Later that night, Julian took us to his flat, a middle class place on top of an old hardware store in Mexico City's downtown. The place was ample and comfortable for his needs, and it wasn't as if he had more belongings besides his vast collection of handicrafts from all over the country and books ranging from science fiction to the occult. An eclectic mix if I had seen one. He asked me to wait in his living room, where most of his books were kept, while he prepared the room he was planning to use for the rite that would prove, at least in his mind, that man was closer to unveiling the secrets of the universe than we thought and that soon, we would rule. Oh, the irony.

It was close to midnight when he was ready and called me to the room. I had almost dozed off reading a book about ancient Egyptian traditions when he asked me to take pen and paper to register his adventure. The room was covered with drawings, sigils and signs that I couldn't recognize, although they seemed to represent spiritual guides called tonas (similar to the familiars in witchcraft traditions) and time and space coordinates, stars and the ilk. They were a mix between pre Columbian styles, Celtic and even prehistoric. But there was something unnerving about them, something that seemed to recall more primordial things. Things that only registered in our collective consciousness as mementos of abject fear. Julian claimed that those sigils were passed from teacher to student for aeons, from the time when the old gods of the Mexican mythology, such as Quetzalcoatl and Tezcatlipoca created this land with sacrifices.

The other thing I noticed was a strong smell of copal, so strong that it almost made me choke. I was then more concerned with dying from being asphyxiated than anything else, so I asked to sit near the door where I could breathe properly. Julian allowed it, despite saying that it was just nonsense. Maybe my closeness to an exit was what helped me in the end.

Julian laid in the bed, surrounded by trinkets and copal burners. As the only modern thing in the room, the clock, struck midnight, he began to recite a sequence of chants composed by words I couldn't make out. Fifteen minutes passed before something changed. It was perhaps the excess of copal in the air, but I could swear that I started to hear a strong sound of drums, banging in a compelling rhythm. I thought I was going to pass out when I saw how the hands of the clock started to move randomly. And it was then when

Julian started to speak in Spanish again to narrate his visions, which I transcribe here:

"It is dark, but not black, the realm beyond the veil. So many sounds and odours. It smells damp and fragrant. I follow the fire of the sun's heart along a current of flowers. I can the dead descending upon the houses of their relatives, eating away the soul offerings on the altar, whispering to their families, words of love or hate. There are dead people that have left much business unfinished and yearn to return to our fleshy cages. I should move from here or else they will try to steal my body like they did with my mentor. I follow the flame… and ah my friend I can do it now, the ebb and flow of time is mine, I can go into the past and visit things that historians ignore and feeble minds avoid."

"I can see our ancestor, yes ours…" To this, I rolled my eyes, "running away from his persecutors, from the Queen's Dragoons into a cave. The cave is deep and I walk alongside him, through a series of tunnels deep into the heart of the land, hoping to fool his enemies. He can hear them, but not see them. Until we hear screams, horrible screams. Something must have happened to the colonial forces. We move swiftly onto another path and what he sees fills our ancestor with dread.

" I don't know how deep we are, the only thing I can see is a line of skeletons, dancing to the sounds of drums, cackling and laughing even if they have no vocal cords, deep and cavernous laughs, going into the deeper innards of the land. And the Spaniards are with them, dancing maniacally, crying, their souls being torn asunder by some strange smoke, their flesh turning into leather, wrapping tightly around their bones. Our ancestor decided to escape before it was too late for him, but I'm protected by these symbols and sigils, so I shall follow them. This is intriguing…."

At this point, I tried to walk up to him and wake him up, regardless of whether what he was saying was true or not. This was taking me down a path that part of me didn't like. However, my limbs felt heavy and I couldn't move more than my hands to keep writing.

"This cave… this cave goes deeper than I thought, not only in space, but in time. I'm going back to the colonial times, into the mines of Guanajuato, when the Spaniards dug for their silver. Ah I see… this cave connects to a mine, the same abandoned mine that collapsed earlier this year. I see the mummies in that museum in the city of Guanajuato. I can hear their screams, their souls trapped in their bodies, slowly eroding, being sucked by a mysterious force."

"I feel I'm being dragged by the flow now. The mummies warn me to resist, but I prefer to know what's deep down. I shall not fall prey to cowardice when I'm so close to finding out…everything. I can feel it in my bones and skin."

By now, I was starting to freak out, but I was feeling disoriented. I could barely do anything else than keep writing, despite my desire to escape the apartment.

"I'm moving so fast, seeing, smelling and tasting the human sacrifices that the Aztec made to the old gods. The historians were wrong. The beating hearts weren't offerings just to keep the sun alight, but to appease something the high priests called the Creature of Bones on the same date we celebrate All Saints' Day, the Day of the Dead. You were right, my friend, our traditions and the others from Ireland and Japan share commonalities, as I can see that folk Celt hero battling the succubus as in the legends. I try to stop and witness the event, but the flow is dragging me faster. The sounds of the drums are almost deafening. Oh heavens! I can see the old gods... Quetzalcoatl the feathered serpent, Tezcatlipoca the black jaguar... Coatlicue... the mother of the four hundred; Huitzilpochtli. The war god the Humming Bird tearing apart his half-sister Coyolxauhqui and using it as a bait for a creature... the same creature of bones.

"The gods are battling it. And then crushing it, but not killing it. I can feel their fear, how they are trapping the creature in the Mictlán, the land of the dead... and the bone peyote is growing from it... I can see them creating the symbols. But they are worthless... damn you Melchor... damn you and your teachings.

"The creature is too strong and has absorbed the Mictlán into it. It has become one with a whole dimension. And the gods are scared. Their folly has polluted the created land as the Creature of Bones now envy the living and yearn for the flesh. The gods seal it deep inside the land and collapse it... but it doesn't matter. I can see the line of skeletons walking happily into its belly, dragging along those foolish Spaniards, into a dance of life and death that takes centuries and seconds at the same time. And they are inviting me… I have to run away!"

By this point, Julian was suffering spasms very similar to those with epilepsy, drenched in sweat and his limbs contorted in positions they weren't meant to do.

"I run as fast as I can. The only exit is towards the future, in another realm. I fight to do it but I finally left behind the drums. I finally can rest, as I'm in the future, a few years from now. The city glows in the dark with all its new buildings. The streets full of movement, like veins full of blood. I can walk freely. It feels like a new place… I follow a cute girl. I can't see her face, but she is slender and dressed in expensive clothing. She moves around as if she owned the city… as if she was the city… Wait… something is wrong. The drums…. I can hear the drums… and see her face… Oh God she is…I must run! This was a mistake! She has Melchor! Oh God!"

And with that, I had enough. Mustering as much strength as I could, I moved my numb limbs to his bed and slapped him hard in the face, several times, until he calmed down. I know that's not the proper way to deal with someone suffering from seizures, but I had enough and I could hear the neighbours downstairs knocking with a broomstick on our floor to make us silent. Julian calmed down and I went to the bathroom to refresh myself. When I came back, Julian was wide awake, sitting at the edge of the bed, mumbling to himself.

I could barely make half of what he said, which I transcribe here too: "Oh God… that's the reason this rite was prohibited. That it shouldn't be mixed with this date and hour nor be used with the bone peyote. That's the reason why the spirits dragged Melchor away in the sandstorm. We are not meant to pierce such realms or they will see us and try to devour us. I'm such an idiot. Man is not meant to know these things or else we will find that we are nothing but meagre entities compared to the Creature of Bones. That's the reason why the natives never dig mines, for fear of awakening the creature of bones that lies deep down in the land.

"The ancient gods created a creature of bones to keep the dead sealed but instead wants to possess the places of the living. They were trapped after witnessing their follies and hubris. The Mictlán is not only a realm, it is a being that yearns to exist in our world. That's what happened with those soldiers in that mine in Guanajuato. That's the reason why there are mummies there. They are not dead, but damned to have their souls drained from their remains for centuries. They are trapped in their decadent bodies, their faces screaming after being trapped in the other world. The urban legends of the place are true. The Spaniards dig too deep and the mines collapsed thanks to a miracle. That is what our ancestor saw in that cave. And these fools are going to awake it again and now it will be too strong to stop it. It knows my scent, it is salivating at the prospect of me being his first meal after a long slumber. I have to stop it!"

Julian then passed into a restless sleep around 2 a.m. I could swear we were there for hours, that it was dawn by now, but the whole experience just took a couple of hours. Julian awoke from his sleep around 3 a.m., on the Second of November, the lesser-regarded Day of the Dead, dedicated to the children and lesser saints. He jumped from his bed and, gathering his sigils, he broke them and created a new one, which he claimed, would protect him in his battle against the creature of bones. I tried to stop him, to force him to rest, as a fever was taking hold of his body and his visage was becoming very pale. But his feverish body showed extraordinary strength and easily pushed me away.

"Keep my diary and the sigils at hand as you could need it. If I fail. But I won't or we will be its slaves forever, dancing in its belly."

He mumbled more incoherent things that only now make sense, before leaving his own flat. I waited for him to come back until the dawn illuminated the now trashed room. But it was to no avail. I placed a call to his cell phone, but the call failed. Tired, I left his flat, closing with his spare keys the front door and avoiding the furious looks of his neighbours that were kept awake thanks to his screams and diatribes. I went to have breakfast in one of those chain restaurants that were open early while I tried to locate him through common friends. Then, I compared his diary with the emails he sent me and I printed, the notes I took the last night and the book 'Of other realities and dreams' and a sense of dread started to fill me.

I went back to the Sonora market, in search of the vendor that sold my friend his ritual apparel, but he was nowhere to be seen. His colleagues mentioned to me how he suddenly fell ill the previous afternoon. I tried to come back to Julian's flat, but for some reason I got lost on several occasions, usually ending in the same lonely street where a beautiful girl with a wide smile waved at me. And when I tried to take the subway, a sense of primal fear stopped me. I was in no mood nor shape to enter the underbelly of the city, which under the light of Julian's visions just gave me a bad feeling. Instead, I took the slower option of buses until I came back to my hotel, picked up my belongings and checked out. I took a cab to the bus station and booked a trip to my hometown. As I was leaving Mexico City behind, I felt as if a great weight was lifted from my shoulders.

However, concern for the well-being of Julian stopped me from enjoying some rest. Once home, I tried to keep my mind busy until the end of the day of the dead, the lesser dead, as I was sure that everything would be fine afterwards. And time eased my soul and I forgot the events of last night. I went out with some other friends, checking my cell phone for news now and then.

It wasn't until a few days later that I realized the true scope of the situation, while reading the newspaper, as there was an article in the cultural section which caught my attention.

During the digging for the new international airport, whose design required very deep foundations, there was an accident that claimed the lives of three construction workers and the leg of a fourth. After the rescue services finished clearing the place, they found the weirdest of things: a mummy, centuries old, not dissimilar to those exhibited in the museum at Guanajuato, holding tightly in his left hand an unknown sigil made of wood and in his right hand, a cane handle made of silver. His face showed a rictus of pain and fear, the mouth wide open.

At first, the experts believed that it might have been the remains of someone buried during the colonial period or even pre- Columbian times that suffered from a process similar to that in Guanajuato. But later, baffled at the contradictions, they discarded it as a hoax and burned it when they found that the rags worn by the mummy were made of synthetic fibres. It didn't make sense, despite the fact that the mummy itself was proven to be centuries old.

At first I didn't care much for the piece of news, until a second look at that sigil filled me with dread and certainty of the fate that fell upon Julian, explaining why he hadn't contacted me by now.

The Creature of Bones was finally here and the veil that kept it sealed away was now closed with it on our side. The sigil and the silver cane were the clue. He was the mummy and they burned him, his mind and soul trapped there, helpless.

I don't know how long I have left, maybe a few days, or maybe I might last a year until the next first of November, when the sound of drums and the illusion of dancing skeletons will trap me. This document shall serve as a record of what happened to Julian. In case it happens to me too. No… I'm certain it will happen to me, no matter how far I move from here, even to another continent. After all, the call from home is too alluring and my mind too open to its call.

Damn you Julian, damn you and your mentor. It knows of me, it is out there, biding its time, walking the city hidden as a beautiful girl with a wide smile. And I know someday, during the Day of the Dead, I will answer its alluring call walking in the middle of the night, mindlessly into the labyrinthine streets until I become lost and sucked out of existence and into the Mictlán, where I will be dancing forever in the belly of the Creature of Bones that is now one with the city.

The city beckons me, the city is now alive and waiting; an eldritch abomination of steel and concrete, glass and asphalt, breathing, waiting, draining… and we are its food.

The Pillar of Hendarac
By Morgan Porter

I awoke, the starless void above me and the wet caked earth below. How long had I been slumbering? A day, a week, longer? I had no reference to gauge the passing of time, no chronometer or moon to track through the heavens, only an inky black space staring back at me. Maybe I was underground. It was possible, but, then, how did I get there?

For that matter, where had I been before I had awakened? I searched my memory and to my horror I found it lacking any useful information as to who I was or what had happened to me. I felt dread and loss, but the causes of such sensations eluded me. The thought of laying in this unknown blackness, waiting for whatever caused my distress to materialize, prompted me to immediate action. I stretched and shuffled to a standing position. There was definitely a ceiling.

The loud crack as my head came into contact with it proved this fact. The sound here was wrong, I screamed and was assaulted by its echo, I could hear my own breath whispering back to me from every dank, dark crevice, every sound was amplified and muffled at the same time. Was it my own breathing or was there something in here with me? I scanned the dark, my eyes finally beginning to adjust to my surroundings – no, nothing in the room with me. Was it a room, a cavern, some jail in the cellar of some long forgotten temple?

I searched my surroundings again. There at the far end, a change in the structure of the wall, a door, the beginning of a hallway, or just a trick of the sickly blue light that was my only illumination.

Wait... Where had the light come from? I looked at the floor and sure enough, I was casting a shadow. The shadow crept off into the room, flickering and jumping as if hunting for its inky brethren or its escape. I looked up, the ceiling itself had begun to glow. Stalactites hung down from the ceiling, humming with eldritch light.

The cavern, for it was indeed a sepulchral place, was filled with these glowing columns of light, hanging from the ceiling or bursting up from the floor like some ancient god's teeth. No, better not to think of this place as a giant mouth, it is just a cave, a cave with eldritch glowing rocks - that is all it is...right?

I picked my way towards the far end where I hoped to find my escape from this eerie place. As I walked, I occasionally tried to break off one of the glowing pillars. Who knew if there would be anything to illuminate the rest of the cave, mouth – no, cave. I finally managed to break off a torch sized piece of one of the stalagmites, it felt cold and clammy. Strange lines of light crisscrossed and danced along its surface.

I stared at these lines transfixed by them for several moments. The lines swirled together into symbols. The symbols writhed and attached themselves to each other, like hagfish in the midst of some slime-covered orgy. Finally, words appeared in the stone, words of a language familiar and yet unknown.

As my eyes ran over the text, visions of a world, again familiar and unknown flitted across my mind's eye. A world of dark blues, greens, and purples, of darkness and strange stars forever streaking across the sky. A world filled with blue and silver-skinned beings working tirelessly in fields of some strange long-stemmed grass with pink fleshy leaves, the leaves waved to and fro in a disjointed and animal-like fashion.

The beings, dressed in attire to match their surroundings, would take clippings from these, for lack of a better word, plants and place them in baskets. I watched as the visions fixed themselves upon a singular being, though I do not know as to why this particular being was of any importance. I watched as the being carried its basket out of the field and into what could only be described as a town in the most figurative of senses. The streets were haphazard and wound around huge boulders and islands of more alien plants, some looking more like stones then living things. The houses, dwellings would be more accurate, were cobbled together from any number of items.

The being I followed moved passed these buildings and up to a gate. It pulled a cord made of some green and coarse fiber, a wheezing burbling noise came from somewhere. A few moments later, the gates opened. This new-found companion of mine, for it seemed as I was not to be leaving its side any time soon, passed through the gates and into a great courtyard.

My companion looked out on a strikingly different scene, the roads here were straight, rocks broken or pushed out of the way to make room for grand avenues, the wild unkempt patches of alien flora were replaced by gardens of delicate ferns or at least fern-like plants. The houses, for these were indeed houses, were constructed of finely chiseled blocks of basalt and gilt in precious stones. A temple stood on the tallest hill in the settlement. This was where my companion was headed. I could feel it.

A sound caught my companion's attention, a terrible roar from above. Looking up, I watched as a monolith fell from the heavens and crushed the top of the temple- no, my companion watched.

The visions stopped. I sat up, apparently having fallen prone at some point during my incursion into my unknown companion's memories, yes memories, of this I was sure, memories of the beginning of a world's apocalypse. I could feel the loss of these strange, unknown and yet familiar beings. My mouth filled with bile,

I retched, as a profound feeling of mourning overcame me, my own or my assuredly dead companion's I could not be sure.

The light from my stalagmite-wrought torch was waning, as was the light emanating from the god's teeth... stone outcroppings, stop that. I reached the aberrant wall I had set out for, the last vestiges of light illuminating the outline of an entrance to a tunnel. I had to bend in half to enter it, my head scrapping against moist and fetid rock.

The smell of putrefaction and rot wafted from some unknown source ahead of me. I clawed my way along the claustrophobic corridor, the scents growing acrid as I crawled closer to what I hoped would be an exit to this place. The corridor gave way to a room of pure black basalt, the one-time inhabitants of the room lay strewn about the floor. I was finally given a proper look at the race that had counted my lost companion as one of its own.

They were hunched beings of a piscean nature. Crests of shimmering bone and scale grew from their skulls. I observed three main body types, whether they denoted sex, age, caste, or similar species of differing biology, I was unable to deduce. The most abundant group, as well as the shortest of the three, wore clothes of a fashion indicative of the same caste or occupation as my lost companion, simple garments of dark blues, greens, and purples.

Their limbs terminated at webbed claws sprouting from doublejointed wrists and ankles, I dubbed them the peasants.

The second-most abundant type found amongst the corpses stood no more than a third my height, and were clad in chitinous armor of a most astounding emerald hue. They carried unusual three-pronged pronged staves of a red stone-like material and nets made from a course green fiber. I tried to remove one of their number's helmets only to find that it was in fact the creature's head and not a helmet at all. I dubbed them the warriors, as that was the most likely of occupations for ones so clad, or was it born or made?

The last group I dubbed the priests, clad in fine apparel and carrying iconography of a most esoteric nature, they varied the most from the other two types in morphology. The priests all looked as if some great hand had decided to remold members of the other two types into mockeries of their former selves.

Tentacles and poorly-wrought fins sprang from wrists and ankles, limbs were bent at impossible angles. The number of eyes and orifices varied from one priest to the next, some lacked both altogether. I picked up one of the warrior's spears, the red stone warm to the touch, the warmth spread through my body and again I felt the world I had become accustomed to fade.

I looked upon the desecrated temple, my spear feeling heavy in my hand as I took in the sheer magnitude of the destruction. The black pillar fell through the darkness as it hummed and wheezed, its mouth - for it indeed had a mouth of a most hideous nature – chewed its way through the temple's roof, ceiling, and entrance hall. I watched as thousands of years of my people's history disappeared in an instant as the accursed thing ate its way through the prayer chambers and priest's cloister.

I could think of nothing but halting its progress to save my city. I jabbed my spear into the side of that foul worm of gray stone skin and black sinew. My aim was true, what followed next made me wish it had not been so. The thing bled a viscous and vitriolic ooze and halted its descent. It screamed again and again, bucking and thrashing as it shrieked in pain. The pillar... worm... nightmarish denizen of the black voids, grew silent, its horrid triple jawed mouth halted its horrid mastication.

Others of the city guard arrived, guardians not warriors, they spread out from my position... my position, no, the guard's position not my own... around the monolithic beast. I watched in horror as one of my brethren came into contact with the creature's blood and fell over gasping, his hand gone at the wrist, the left side of his face melted as if by intense heat or acid. I watched as his body dissolved into nothingness before my eyes.

There was a whispering sound, a whining noise belonging to no creature I could identify, coming from above. A yellow being of a sleek build hummed as it circled the columnar abomination. It propelled itself through the heavens using no anatomy recognizable to me or any of my brethren. The area had become too foul with the blood of the beast for any of us to dare stay with in close proximity to it.

The yellow creature's eye glowed red as it spied the incapacitating wound to its master, minion, mate? The yellow creature made clicking noises and spun on its axis. We took cover, fearing this new being might be looking to avenge its stricken comrade. It circled out from its original position, clicking and humming as it glided on unseen forces around the site of its partner's devastating attack. I watched it from my hidden vantage point as it flew over the rubble that had once been the temple, I followed its progress and, for the first time, saw the sheer magnitude of the damage done to my city... the guard's city- the host's thoughts and feelings were blurring with my own...

The houses surrounding the temple lay in ruin, rubble choked causeways and avenues, gardens laid dead or dying from exposure to the worm's caustic blood.

The yellow creature spiraled back up into the heavens. A few of my fellow guards argued for giving chase, others argued for the evacuation of the city, still others argued for the rescue of the priests trapped on the lower floors of the temple. The priests would surely be able to offer answers as to what these malevolent beings were and what might appease them. I followed, voiceless and powerless, a shade on the guard's shoulder, as we backtracked towards that ruined shrine and its presumably dead violator.

There was death all around us, a scale of destruction the likes of which I had never seen... I had never seen, this was not a statement I could lead any credence too, as I could not remember anything before waking up in that thrice-damned cavern...

I watched as gear was collected, rubble was removed and a small tunnel was dug into the lower sanctums of the temple.

The lower chambers were miraculously saved from the destruction above, if not for the frantic scurrying of the priests, one would not suspect that the floors above no longer existed. We wandered the halls, my eyes gliding over the strange pictographs etched on to every conceivable flat space.

I deduced that these pictographs were some sort of history or holy text. They depicted all manner of being, some of impossible proportions. A mural graced the wall across from us at an intersection, a creature looking like one of the peasants, only of such grandiose stature as to dwarf the likeness of the temple depicted beneath it, fought a thing with five arms and five eyes.

I felt an odd kinship to the giant piscean being. I felt a sense of purpose flow through my new companion, removing all fear and worry. I watched through unblinking eyes as the same calm came over the other guard. We walked into the inner sanctum of the temple. Priests of every rank and deformity chanted whilst facing three statues in the center of the chamber.

Two shared their likenesses with that of the creature I had seen in the mural, though one was obviously female. The third was of a more striking countenance, its jaws were wreathed in tentacles, its two arms ended in clawed hands, fins of a Potanichthys nature sprouted from between its massive shoulder blades.

The guard I shadowed, as well as his comrade, walked through the mass of chanting priests up to the statues and genuflected in front of the creature from the mural's likeness. A wet gargling noise came from my left, the head priest had sliced the throat of our comrade. I was unable to help, unable to scream, as I felt that obsidian blade draw across my host's neck, inexplicably the only things I felt from him as he lay dying were sensations of peace and duty fulfilled.

I found myself once again in that charnel chamber, my back sticky with some noxious goo. I realized to my revulsion that I had fallen into a pile of offal and excrement, I was stained with the blood of dozens of these beings. I took a moment to collect my thoughts, it was becoming more and more difficult to separate my own point of view and emotions from those of my dead companions. I was here in this place and time but part of me still felt as if it was with my two dead companions watching as their world came to a violent end.

I looked upon the scene with fresh eyes, this was not a butchering or an act of mercy, this was a sacrifice, a last attempt to appease or perhaps punish the invaders who had wrought such destruction upon the city. I inspected those corpses nearest me and was given credence for my hypothesis, all of them had had their throats slit from behind.

I found a strange glowing fungus in a large basalt bowl in corner of the chamber, I scanned the wall and realized these bowls were at regular intervals and used for illumination. Eager to have a light source of my own yet wary of touching the alien spore I stabbed a piece with the spear I still carried and made every attempt not to stare directly at the soft orange glow.

I went further into the chamber and came face to face with those statues from my visions. The Tentacled One and the female lay toppled on the floor of the chamber, the male Piscean God stood alone, its eyes, two pieces of obsidian, stared down upon the abominable beast that lay at its webbed feet.

The beast's head was encased within a yellow shell, its Cyclopean eye was dark and glassy and stared unblinking at the ceiling, its paws were small and useless lacking any sort of nail or claw, while its long hind quarters truncated in long black fins, this must have been one of the Pillar Worm's disciples, or possibly the disciple of the Yellow One.

I looked down on the face of this malformed creature from the heavens, its mouth, at least it would be where a mouth would be on any sane creature of similar bilateral construction, was filled with probosces all running from a central echinoderm-like disk. Its skin was a light blue and looked rubbery to the touch. I left it there, I did not wish to touch it as I had no desire to have visions of whatever hellish planescape from which this being had escaped.

I followed the wall to the door I had seen in my visions and as a flesh and bone being, I navigated those labyrinthine tunnels that I had only seen in the memories of that dead piscean guard. The corridors were cramped and made harder to traverse by collapsed walls and scattered debris. I came once again to that intersection and the mural on the wall opposite had changed. No longer were the Piscean God and that five-eyed horror locked in eternal combat, instead The Pillar Worm, here looking more serpentine then annelid and surrounded by tiny one-eyed blue beings and accompanied by that accursed Yellow One, rained fire and destruction down upon the temple and the city, of the Piscean God there was no sign. I wondered at this, had their god abandoned them, had he been killed?

As I stared at the mural longer, a sound from down one of the halls caught my attention. A grinding gurgling sound, a sound so terrible and so familiar it froze me where I stood. The Pillar Worm was still in the temple and I was in here with it.

I fought the urge to flee, I had no idea how close the thing was, nor whether it could sense my presence. I could not be sure I was not hallucinating. Who knew what the effect of sharing in the last memories of a dead being has on the thought patterns of a living one?

I calmed myself, I tried to find peace in that mural again, this time I only found sorrow and rage in equal parts. I felt the emotional weight of an entire species crying out against its own extinction.

I felt the anger of an entire species as it fought tooth and claw against an uncaring alien exterminator. I could feel my fists pound against the walls, a howl of infinite fury and mourning forced its way out through my rictus-clenched jaws, in that moment I cared not if the Pillar Worm heard me or not. I wanted it to come. I wanted to end it, either it or I would die, it did not matter which, there would be closure for one of us.

I followed that hideous noise to its source. The Pillar Worm stood in what was left of the temple's central chamber, it had grown an exoskeleton since the last time I had laid eyes upon it. I saw the Yellow One surrounded by six of its yellow shelled disciples, they belched streams of noxious gases as they circled their master.

I watched as one of the disciples pulled away from the Yellow One and swam towards the Pillar Worm. The disciple burbled something I could not make out, and covered its head with its one shriveled claw and with the other it pointed at the Pillar Worm, I now know why it had such small and useless paws, it did not need nails or claws to protect itself, it could call forth lava to spew from its very fingertips.

It bore down on the Pillar Worm's exoskeleton, melting bits of it and fusing rods of an unknown material into the exoskeleton's architecture. Were they helping or hindering the abomination? I wondered was it an exoskeleton or a cage? Had the Yellow One been the Pillar Worm's jailer all along? Could I have misread the relationship between the two so badly? It did not matter, they and their disciples were all responsible for the cataclysm that had ended this once great civilization.

My memories returned in a sudden rush, clarity finally came to me as I readied myself for combat. I stretched my claws, extended the venomous spines from my elbows and dorsal fin, I unhinged my lower jaw and brought my tusks to bare in front of my fangs. I had failed my people, I had let Da'sho'yhgat fall to these defilers. I had in my hubris thought my people beyond the reach of any threat, and left them to their fate to pursue other matters. I lifted my head and bellowed.

I rammed the Yellow One with all of my strength, I rammed my spear into its yellow unyielding flesh. I heard a shriek of surprise from the abomination as I bore it to the ground beneath me.

Lava and eldritch energy spewed from the fissure I had created, searing my limbs and cooking the scales from my chest. I heard the Yellow One screech and implode, the implosion mangling my legs and shattering my right eye socket. I lost myself then, screaming into the darkness, my mind, soul, and body dissolving into the Æthers as time lost its grip upon me.

I awoke, the starless void above me and the wet caked earth below. How long had I been slumbering? A day, a week, longer?

Beast

By Alei Kotdaishura

When she arrived to the office, she was pale and puffy-eyed. "You look like a mess," her boss said as a greeting. "Are you alright?" She denied silently. "I woke up this morning feeling nauseous. It might have been yesterday's dinner," she explained. She had always been pale-skinned and puffy-eyed, but this time she looked worse than usual.

The previous night, her boss had invited her to dinner surprising everyone, for he had a reputation as a greedy man with a nasty temper. He had also been a jerk to her for over a week, to the point that he had even bragged loudly that were it not for him, she would be dead by now.

She'd planned a trip to the lake with her folks. Unfortunately, that Friday her boss had harangued her into staying. "There is just too much to be done in the office," he concluded. "I need you here."

Grudgingly, she stayed – if she hurried, she might be able to reach them late Saturday. Meanwhile, her boss left early Friday with a backpack and a mocking smile.

Her parents had gone ahead to the lake without her. She felt alone and overwhelmed at the office, under the dim lights, working at a slower rate than she had expected. Still at the office, she got the call late Saturday afternoon on her cell from an officer who had been as gentle as possible: her parents had been in a wreck. Afterwards, she couldn't even end the call. The phone slipped out of her hand — she cried for the rest of the night and into Sunday morning.

Even while arranging the funeral, her boss wouldn't let her ease up on her workload. "It has to get done," he told her. Whenever she tried to face him about him being a jerk, he justified his actions. "I saved your life last weekend, why should I take it easy on you?"

She had gone to the dinner to try to cheer herself up, but it hadn't helped: the sickness had been a hard way to finish an already difficult day. Still, what she didn't say was that her sickness had been mixed with an awful night full of nightmarish dreams that she couldn't remember at all except for the strange silhouettes with some kind of skin patches, dark against dull light in a forest.

As she got through the days, her boss kept bullying her.

"You're not working as well as you did before. What are you, stupid?"

"You don't seem to understand my instructions; do I need to repeat it a third time?"

"Hurry up! I needed that order two hours ago and you don't seem to have started yet!"

With every remark, she felt worse and worse. Her sickness was not helping and she felt like crying, but she managed to hold on until she got home that night. She closed the door behind her and cried, missing her parents.

Along with the strange silhouettes, she began hearing a voice. It was deep, and it could have been described as one of those seductive radio voices, were it not for its strange resemblance to her boss's, making her skin crawl when it should have enticed her. It kept talking through her dreams, waking her up once and again, shivering in fear, even though she couldn't understand what it was saying.

The next day began cloudy and rainy, although it was the middle of summer. This did nothing to improve her mood and her sickness.

Apparently, the bad weather was tuned to her boss, who was even nastier than before, as if the dinner invitation had been a lapse in his awful behavior.

"Am I surrounded by idiots? Does anyone understand what I'm asking? Certainly you don't." He said pointing at her after asking loudly to the rest of the department. No one had dared to answer him or even turn to look at her.

"I don't want a crappy report. If it is not excellent, don't even bring it in here." He told her, looking at his computer's screen without even seeing her reports when she showed up at his office.

And it kept going. By the end of the day she was jumpy and fearful to even leave her seat, but she didn't want to stay either.

The night didn't bring any comfort. She was even more tired than the day before, but now she was fearful of her dreams. Two full nights of unremembered nightmares in a row after two days of bullying pushed her limits. Still, she didn't have a choice and she went to sleep, praying that she would have a dreamless night. But she didn't.

During the days that followed, she kept hearing the dream voice again and again. In the daytime, whenever she remembered the dream voice, she got goosebumps, for the voice drew her into some dreamy state, entrancing her. Whenever it whispered in her dreams, she felt her spirit being seduced and filled with the voice, not quite pleasantly but neither totally unpleasant, although it did leave a void when it remained silent during the dreams, gradually making her feel like an addict, even if the voice filled her with dread as well as pleasure.

Her wakeful hours weren't much better. The sickness increased and she started losing weight and her focus on her work. Her boss noticed almost immediately and his bullying became worse as her health degraded, almost becoming menacing and raging.

"You're so narrow-minded. I need you to think bigger and better or everyone else will be promoted before you finish your work," he screamed at her in the middle of the office.

"How could you think this would work? You're not even following the company guidelines," he would say at times, throwing her reports to her face when she did her best to present creative proposals.

She wished more and more that she could run away from the office and hide at her place as soon as possible, especially after the sneers and looks of contempt she got form her coworkers. Not having somewhere or someone to turn to, she could do nothing else but cry silently in her apartment and pray that this wasn't punishment for not being able to see her parents one last time before they died.

The dreams increased their intensity, the dream voice getting clearer and more frightening every night, becoming more and more like her boss's voice, and the dream silhouettes becoming more detailed. At first they were animals, and she gradually understood that the dreams were about her hunting and feeding off of them, all of them ordered by the dream voice. Those dreams filled her with terror, for at the beginning of each she got an adrenalin surge from the hunt that she interpreted as freedom. She relished the feeling of flesh tearing in her mouth, filling her with warm blood and warm, tasty meat. But then, the pleasure turned into terror as the voice laughed, enjoying her pleasure, and she understood that she was being manipulated and she couldn't stop it.

The freedom she felt at night left her numb during the day.

"You're no good at this and no one will hire you if you leave, so be thankful you still have a job." He said to her one day. She just nodded and left to her desk. She didn't even care anymore what happened at work. At night, she would have her release.

As the nights passed, the animals began to take human forms: girls, boys, men, women, babies, Asian, Black, White, Latin... as the dreams progressed, she felt that voice calling her again and again, compelling her and forcing her to chase the humans, haunting them at first to feed from their fear and, when it became terror and drove them to madness, hunting them and killing them. The scenarios changed: sometimes she was in villages, towns or cities, sometimes in forests, deserts, pastures… but the dreams were always the same: haunt, hunt, kill, feed and gorge, haunt, hunt, kill, feed and gorge.

After every dream, she was more scared, waking up and dreading going back to sleep, hoping the dreams wouldn't return, and then repeating the cycle again and again all night.

"You're the weakest link in this department; do I have to get in your head to fix you?" Her boss said one day. She hung her head low in order to look contrite, but remained silent. She started wishing she lived in her dreams. They weren't much better and filled her with terror, but she also felt free, and she craved that feeling.

The dreams continued to evolve. Now, before she started the haunting cycles, her skin started to melt, transforming itself into different animals. Sometimes it was a lynx, a wolverine, a lion, a tiger, a panther; others it was a goat, a bear, a dog, or a mix of several animals at the same time, all badly sewn together, the stitches marking on the skin haphazardly. After awakening, she began checking her skin under the light, and gradually she began noticing scars in her legs and torso where they weren't before, seeming like badly a sewn costume.

These days, her sickness was her normal self. She began her days feeling guilty, terrified, nauseous and dizzy. She could barely keep her focus anymore and she didn't care much for her own health. She had become a skinny creature with eyes that reminded everyone of a raccoon or a panda, so dark were the circles around them.

"I can't stand your mediocrity," began her boss one day after she arrived into the office. "If you don't want this job, I can find someone better out there. In fact, take your things and leave, I don't need you and no one else will ever." She kept staring at him for a minute more, and left quietly. For a moment, she considered packing her few personal belongings before leaving, but she really didn't care much for them, and somehow she felt she would not need them any time soon.

She went home and opened the fridge to eat, staring blankly inside. She barely ate anymore, and when she did, it was mechanical and absent-mindedly, so she hadn't noticed that her feeding habits were changing, sometimes eating with her hands, or sitting in strange animal postures. This time, she didn't notice she was eating raw meat until it was almost over and she screamed, throwing away the meat. She ran into the bathroom, intending to vomit, and stopped in front of the mirror. She stared at her reflection, shaking and noticing with dread the difference in her looks; while the dream voice, clear and enticing, whispered to her that it didn't matter anymore.

A chill ran down her back. The voice had never whispered to her while she was awake and she understood her time was running out.

She locked herself in her bedroom, the curtains closed so the sun didn't bother her, and she cried in desperation, asking her parents for forgiveness for not being able to be there one last time, until she fell asleep. That night the dream was different, for it had the quality of a memory.

* * *

The day after she was told that her parents had died she had been unable to cope with her overflowing sadness and stress, waking up shortly after midnight. So restless that she couldn't go back to sleep, she dressed and went out to pace into the nearby woods, hoping the fresh night air would relax her.

She had paced for what seemed like hours, going deeper into the woods without a single soul disturbing her, either animal or human.

Suddenly, she heard the rustle of bushes and felt creepy eyes watching her. She turned around but saw no one. She kept pacing a bit further until she felt more acutely those eyes on her, predatory and malevolent.

A chill ran through her back and she ran, instinctively trying to get away from her observer. She ran for at least twenty minutes before starting to tire. Finally she stopped and bent over out of breath, her hands hanging on her knees, shaking. Safe, she thought. But the feeling didn't last.

Before she had time to react, something pounced on her back from between two trees. The creature had a cloyingly musky smell, but it also smelled of filth and death. She felt the creature breathing heavily over her, smelling her deeply from her nape to her buttocks.

She tried to move, scared, but couldn't shake the creature from her back. Suddenly, she felt the creature snarling and rubbing itself against her, as if marking her with its scent. She stifled a scream and tried to stay quiet, but it didn't help.

The creature turned her over with one long and sharp-clawed paw, scratching her shoulders and her torso while doing so. She tried to take a look at the creature, but it was so dark she only saw yellow teeth and dark shiny eyes, with red rings around its pupils. She closed her eyes and prayed her death would come fast. The creature repeated the smelling and rubbing, placing its paws over her arms to immobilize her, this time going from her neck to her crotch. Its breath stank of a mixture of something rotten, dry leaves and decaying forest. She trembled and remained still, waiting for the creature to kill her until she felt dizzy and lost consciousness.

She awoke in the morning, the sun shining on her face, daylight pouring through her curtained window. She jolted from bed and ran to the bathroom to check the places where the creature had scratched her, but there were none – no scratches, bruises or marks at all, so she had concluded it had been one hell of a nightmare.

* * *

Tonight the dream memory left her feeling dizzy, fevered and more scared than ever. She had goosebumps on her whole body. She felt restless. It was past midnight already, just like that night, but the voice compelled her to get dressed and to take a walk in the nearby forest. She complied, not even trying to resist it. Come… it whispered. Come to me…

She went into the woods, shivering. It was beginning to chill, and she realized it was middle autumn already. She dove deep into the wilderness, beyond what common sense suggested as a safe area at night, following the voice's commands. She heard the wind ruffling the trees and the wild night animals.

She couldn't get out of her system the uneasiness that the dream memory had left her. Suddenly, she realized that she was being watched, just like that night. She thought she sensed someone's heavy breathing, deeper than the wind between the trees.

Remembering her dream, she started running in a panic, until she exhausted herself, reaching the riverbed. She sat down on some rocks unable to continue, and tried to calm her breath hoping that she had lost whatever creature that had been watching her.

She heard footsteps coming her way, crunching some branches and dry leaves. She tried to get up, but her legs didn't respond, as if they no longer belonged to her. The footsteps were heavy and slow, even dragging a bit. Finally, she saw the silhouette of a man coming out of the woods and stepping into the moonlight.

She gasped. Although it had a human silhouette, up close it didn't seem to be human. The few clothes it wore seemed to suggest it had been human once, more than actually using them to protect itself from the chilly autumn air. It had long and shaggy hair on its head and back, its skin looked flayed in some parts, sewn back together, forming patches here and there, the arms longer than a human's. And the face! It seemed to have no nose but a misshapen tumor on the center, with wild, dark eyes rimmed with a red glow. The skin looked melted, just like the one in her nightmares.

She trembled, paralyzed. As the chimera came closer, she noticed that all its body seemed to be covered in scars where the skin was patched and multicolored, but it seemed to be healing. She felt pain in her body and she turned to look at her arms. The skin was changing faster than the days before, becoming a patchwork just like the chimera's. As she turned to watch the approaching monster, she noticed the patches on its arms were disappearing, as if they were transferring onto hers. She turned a puzzled look towards the chimera's face and saw a savage grin on what could be called its mouth.

"Scared of what you see, hun? Disgusted?" For a moment, she didn't understand what she was hearing. It was her dream voice, but it didn't come from the creature before her, it was coming from some other place.

The voice laughed hard. As it talked, the voice's owner came out of the woods to her left and she gasped as she found herself in front of her boss.

"I've been looking for a pet replacement for a while now," he explained, while the chimera was turning into a man in his midtwenties, his face still distorted, but now regaining its former handsomeness, except for a relieved expression that made the change look surreal.

"I'm a demon that feeds from fear and remorse, and you have given me enough of both," he continued. His voice was seductive, and she shivered with pleasure, regardless of his hideous speech. "I may have killed your parents. I might have made your life a living hell, but I saw that you were already full of grief – you were already my victim. All I did was show you your weakness."

He laughed loudly, his voice reverberating in the empty forest.

She looked at him, enraptured.

"Now, it's time for the final stage of the change," he kept going.

"Welcome, my pet!"

He turned to look at her. She screamed until her throat was rough, and then she screamed more and more while she felt the last of her transformation. The scars and patches crawled in her skin, feeling like invisible vermin. Her face melted and changed, turning into a hideous mass of warts and tumors. Her thin mouth distorted and her teeth turned, some into stone, others into fangs. Her hands became claws and her feet grew huge, turning into paws. Her back distorted, forcing her to become four footed, with an ape-like appendage between her legs that could pass for a tail. Finally, her hair grew longer and thicker.

The new chimera shook out of her remaining clothes and turned to look at the monster turned into a man, who was laughing in relief after being freed from his chimera body. The demon boss turned to look at her new form and ordered her.

"Now run! Enjoy you last moments of sanity before becoming a full beast. I will call you and control you, and you will remain that way until you are useless to me!"

She relished the change and growled in bliss, thanking the full moon for freeing her from her grief. She turned to her demon boss and the former chimera, raising a mighty claw and swiping down at them, managing a few last words.

"I am free!"

The Server of Souls
By Brent A. Harris

I became aware. My eyes flicked open and I scanned my surroundings. Sun streamed in through fresh, white blinds and reflected off the sterile tile floor surrounding my hospital bed.

Everything was a reflection. In the back of my memory, I heard something distant and vague—almost like an echo. Darkness started closing around my periphery, yet visions of loved ones passed through my sight. There was a high-pitched scream from my eight-year-old girl, followed by a sensation of falling. And then everything was stilled by a rhythmic beeping of a heart monitor.

My first thought was that I might have had amnesia. But if I did, it proved to be selective: My name was Richard Rigby, I lived on Mesa Drive near Phoenix. I was a computer programmer and inventor, though my inventions only lived within the processors of a machine. No, I hadn't lost all of my memory, despite how forgetful and forgettable I had been.

I had attempted to invent something quite novel, something that could have changed the way we perceived our world. I had tried to cheat death. If I had succeeded, everybody could have lived forever.

My program, my invention, would have made us all gods. But somehow, I was stuck in a hospital bed, with no way of knowing what had happened to me.

The door to my room finally opened and a woman walked in. I sucked in an air of surprise when I recognized something familiar about her—she had my small round nose and brown hair, though hers was long and wavy and mine… I did not know how my hair looked anymore. Fortunately, she did not have my plain brown eyes.

She had her mother's green ones. I exhaled relief; it was my daughter, Ellie, older now. I had begun to smile, but when I saw the sadness behind her sullen expression, my smile turned into a frown.

"Dad… it's time we talked." She refused to look me in the eye.

Ellie took the clipboard at the foot of the bed and scanned it over.

"Let's go, we can talk in the car," She spoke matter-of-factly. Her coat was still draped over her arm in front of her, as if not expecting to stay, as if I was going to get up right now and walk out of here…

That didn't make sense. None of this did. This was not my little girl and I didn't even know if I could have stood. She had grown.

And she seemed… absent, oblivious to my condition. Obviously, I must have been in a coma; time had passed. I stretched back into my memory, brow furrowing in thought. I could not remember how I had gotten here. I had to have been gone for a while. But for how long?

I don't particularly remember Richard Rigby—that man I once was so long ago—to be an overly courageous type. That was my wife. And my daughter. When Ellie was sick in the hospital with pneumonia, with all those needles and tubes in her, she was so brave and strong. And then when my wife was in the hospital. She was strong—even till the end.

I mustered up the strength and asked Ellie, "How long have I been gone?"

She either didn't hear me, or she ignored me. Either way, she said nothing at all.

* * *

I was in the car now, a polished silver bullet from what I thought the future would look like. It floated above the road, like a cloud. I don't remember how I had gotten there, but I was tethered down, buckled into the backseat. Ellie was beside me. That made me glad.

Since there was no one driving the car, we should have been able to talk. But she was silent. And I was trapped inside my thoughts.

My periphery began to fade again, my senses suddenly dulled.

Only this time, I saw a streak of smoke in the air, as if coming from a small aircraft. The black-grey streak continued—violently, it descended from the clouds to the hell below.

Then there was a sensation of falling again. As if the car disengaged from the mag-track and rolled end-over-end down a steep ravine. I heard that high-pitched scream again blowing through my ears. I grasped instinctively for Ellie, and I saw her young again, but I could not hold onto her. Then, it stopped, except for the beeping of the heart monitor, that omnipresent persisting rhythm— was it trying to signal someone? A flash of a memory overwhelmed me... Ellie and I were in a car. My prototype was with us. We were on the way to test it, to see if I could get it to—

"You know it worked, right?" Ellie interrupted my thoughts.

Everything was still again. At first I was angry, I wanted to remember, I was so close to remembering! But then I took a breath and relaxed. I was grateful for the interruption. I wanted to hear my daughter again. It had been so long. I waited in silence, hoping she would continue.

"I know you did it for Mom." She stared out the window, off into the distance, where I had seen the trail of grey-black smoke only moments ago. "You did it for the one person you needed most, the one person your device could never have worked for." There was anger in her voice now, her hands squeezing the car cushion. "And I lost everything because of it." She squeezed harder, "But your device worked and now we don't lose anybody at all, right? So we are never alone." She stifled a laugh that turned into a sniffle as tears began a slow descent down her cheeks.

Her eyes grew small, as if sinking into her sockets, it was wearing me down. She continued, even though now I wished she might stop.

"I only wanted to spend time with you, to be your daughter. I begged you to take me with you that night. And of course, I lost both of my parents then." She sobbed openly. I wanted to comfort her, as a father should for his daughter, but I was helpless. I couldn't even remember what she was talking about. "I'm alright. I'm alright now, but if I ever want to heal, to move on, I have to let you go."

I tried to search my memory of the night she referred to. I remembered being in my car, a rusted silver sedan, in the rain. But all I saw were flashes, as some senses faded and others grew stronger. Finally, different scenes flickered past: I saw my wife, lowered into a grave, alone. Then I recalled the sudden death of my dad. I had witnessed first-hand the horrors of loss, all I wished to do was to stop it. I wanted to save him—to save them all—to use my device, even though I knew it was a lie. The Rigby Device cannot save them. It doesn't work. It... cannot work. We are all doomed to die alone.

My thoughts vanished as the car bounced off the mag-track onto the driveway. The wheels hit the ground like an airplane landing. I was no longer in the clouds. I was home. The house hadn't changed.

I was inside now, though I wasn't quite sure how I had gotten here.

But I found myself in my familiar study. The computer desk was over in the corner, wires sticking out of it. There was the soft white-blue brilliance of the monitor as programs processed. My eight-year-old was excitedly talking. I nodded half-heartedly in response. She seemed to be happy, as if I had agreed to something.

The wind rustled leaves against the window. The storm was getting stronger now. And then I was back to where it all began. The hum of the CPU, the whir of the fan. I was surrounded by the musty smell of old books. I loved it. The feel of the pages, the weight of the words in my hand. I loved books the way I loved the feel of fingers clapping across a keyboard. But I turned away from the shelves. My gaze was towards the computer. The first Rigby Device was plugged into it. The black box, no thicker than an average-sized hardback, clicked to life. Outside, lightning flickered. Thunder followed without pause.

"Goodbye, father," my daughter said softly. "It's time for me to be alone," her voice was an echo, fading away.

My heart had sunk with those words. And then, I was alone. My mind was back in the present. The musty books were gone. The shelves were there, but they were nearly empty, except for a few unrecognizable electronic devices and a few book-thick black boxes.

I felt the dark closing in on me again. A fading shroud pulsated around me. Now, I was enveloped in the grey-black streak of smoke I had seen before. I felt the sensation of falling again, and I heard

Ellie scream once more. I wanted to run to her... but she was gone—nothing was left except for the rhythmic haunting of the heart monitor as it continued its merciless alert. I heard each and every beep. I started to feel afraid. I wanted to understand what was happening. I wanted the fading to stop, I wanted—

I looked in disbelief. Before me was a man, who certainly should not have been there. My heart jumped a beat, and the beeping and tumbling halted. I stared into his graying hair and gray-blue eyes. He didn't look any different from the last moment I had seen him. I whispered..., "Dad?"

* * *

"You act surprised to see me," He spoke in a deep voice, deeper than I remembered. "After all," my father continued, "this is your invention. Surely you envisioned an improvement upon your original design? There's been advances while you were gone. Advances in cloning and bio-electrics." He put his hand on my shoulder. It was warm, but it lacked reassurance. "You helped change the world, son. The box was only the beginning."

While everything in front of me remained sharp, the images in my periphery were becoming increasingly grey and foggy. I didn't understand. Where was my daughter? My dead father was standing here, unchanged in age, detached in feeling. I needed answers. I needed them now. I had the sense of falling again, and I heard the damned heart monitor. This had to stop. I had to kn—

"What the hell happened to me?"

"You… are dead." My father took a deep breath and stuffed his hands back into his leather flight jacket. With a frown he said, "You know you never survived the car accident, right? Just like I died in that plane crash."

The trail of smoke descending from the clouds. I remembered.

Then, another brief flash of memory struck me, like a lightning strike. I witnessed my own death. I was back in my car again, on the way to my lab. My daughter was with me, I had her strapped into the backseat. My device, the black box, sat on the passenger seat beside me. The pattering rain that had started while we were back at the house had become a monsoon. The desert roads were slick with oil and water. It was dark; black clouds blocked out the stars. Then, a flash-flood hit us. The sudden surging river rolled over my sedan, shoving us off the road. It took us tumbling down the ravine of the small mountain pass. We fell for what seemed forever, down the dirt, end over end.

My daughter... my young daughter, screamed in terror the whole time. But there was nothing I could do for her, no comfort I could give. I shuddered, then shrank back with horror. My father must have caught my reaction, for he said in a stern voice, "You don't need to worry about Ellie anymore."

He shook his head and paced around the empty shelves of the library in my home. "You were fortunate that you decided to implant your conscious into your device to test it when you did. Your work was intact and you became the inadvertent poster-boy for immortality. The Rigby Device was born. He slipped into a slick salesman's voice, as if in mockery, "You never have to be alone again. Keep your loved ones with you forever."

He moved his arm in an arc in front of him as the advertisement rolled out of his mouth.

Pieces of my memory came back to me, though I had no memory of anything beyond the accident and the beeping of the heart monitor. I remembered working on the programming for the device.

The frustration. The empty K-cups. My daughter, begging to play. I remembered that I failed. But my daughter was so proud of me. She knew if I finished… I'd have more time. And I knew, if I finished, succeeded, then I'd never have to leave her, she'd never be alone.

So, I redoubled my efforts, grabbed my faulty prototype and took her with me to work in my lab that night. And then I remembered nothing…

"B-but I just woke up in the hospital, we took a car ride over here—"

"Who knows what that was?" His eyebrows rose, as if he were not telling me everything, "You have been active for decades." His voice lowered in concern, "Are you sure you have no memory of those years?"

"No."

"Strange… strange indeed."

"So it worked, my device… worked?"

"No."

And that's when the truth spilled out, everything became revealed.

My father let loose, raising his voice, "You were a deceiver. You sold false hope. You convinced a world that your brain was stuffed in a box." He took a breath and pointed an angry finger at me.

"You were never able to download a mind. It's all a bunch of 1's and 0's. It was search engine parameters, old social media posts, and psych profiles. Unless you have servers full of souls locked away in the basement computer room at Rigby Enterprises, you are a snake-oil salesman."

"I didn't do any of that," I stammered out. "I was in a box six feet underground, as you said." I wanted to pace around the library, but I stood still. Instead, slowly I said, "I… died."

"Ah, but you didn't. At least, you refused to believe you had. You seemed very much alive inside that box of yours. You passed the Turing test... every test every programmer made for you. You made people believe—you made your daughter believe!" Grey-black smoke coalesced around him. He had begun to smell of fire and ash.

"But you and I know the truth, now don't we?"

"That's... not possible. None of this is," I assured my father. "It doesn't even make sense." My own death flashed before me. I heard my daughter's scream. But I knew nothing from after the accident. I wanted to ball my fists in fury. My logical programmer-brain wanted to understand. "If I downloaded my conscience into this machine before my death, then how do I remember it?"

My father was quiet for a few beats of a still heart. When he finally spoke, his face told me he had no further answers, "This could all be in your head. Perhaps you're in your hospital bed, slipping away and this is your mind fighting its finality." He took a step closer and lowered his voice to an eerie calm. "But, remember, you designed the box much like a phone, with a camera, a microphone... connection to the internet. Maybe that box of yours recorded the event. Or…" Then he gave a wicked smile, "Could it be, maybe, you've reached awareness? Perhaps, after decades, all those 1's and 0's clicked into consciousness. Maybe there is a soul in there, after all."

Then, his smile disappeared and that beeping from the heart monitor returned, although faded, as if it were dying down.

"You wanted to live on, to become a god. You tried to cheat death, to steal souls away in your servers. But nobody lasts forever. We all fade. He raised his finger at me again, although this time, his finger rotted away to yellow-black bone as he said, "it looks like you almost got your wish. You'll live on forever in this machine of yours." Then he smiled wickedly, and laughed as he finished, "or at least until your battery runs out."

Smoke surrounded my father as he faded away, his laughter echoed in the back of my mind. As he disappeared, the ever-present beeping continued to weaken. Or, perhaps it was me who was fading away. I had the sudden sinking feeling that I was dying—all over again. I didn't understand, I need to see

Ellie, I needed to be with my daughter one more time. Where was she?

I searched around, all I saw were discarded books, a dusty shelf, circuits and wires. I heard the hum of the CPU, the whir of the fan. It wasn't my computer. It was me. This can't be. I'm not just a computer program, I'm alive. "I'm alive!" I screamed. I kicked and pounded at the black tin wall before me. "This is really me. I'm really here, Ellie, don't you hear me? This is your father, I'm alive!"

My view of the near-empty bookshelf grew dark. And then the once rhythmic beeping of the low battery alert slowly faded away…

Afterword

Thank you for reading, we hope you enjoyed the taste of fantasy – we hope you shivered along with fear!

Inklings Press aims to offer a platform for new writers. As well as the double anthology you hold in your hands, we have published three more collections – Tales From The Universe soars into the worlds of sci-fi, Tales From Alternate Earths looks at how the world might have turned out if history had taken a different twist, and our latest, Tales of Wonder, embraces the realm of science fantasy in which the likes of Star Wars and steampunk rub shoulders.

We'd love to hear from you – you can tweet to us @inklingspress, or visit our website, www.inklingspress.com. You can also find details there to sign up for a regular newsletter, keeping you up to date with all the latest information on upcoming publications, discount deals and more.

We're also on Facebook at www.facebook.com/inklingspress.

We'd also love you to share with others what you thought of the anthology – so we'd heartily encourage you to add your reviews to Amazon, Goodreads or wherever readers dwell.

Our first year was quite a year – we can't wait to show you what we've got lined up for the future!

Made in the USA
San Bernardino, CA
30 March 2017